MMXV

THE WHITE REVIEW

EDITORS	BENJAMIN EASTHAM & JACQUES TESTARD
DESIGN, ART DIRECTION	RAY O'MEARA
POETRY EDITOR	J. S. TENNANT
US EDITOR	TYLER CURTIS
ASSOCIATE EDITOR	FRANCESCA WADE
ASSISTANT EDITOR	HARRY THORNE
EDITORIAL ASSISTANT	CASSIE DAVIES
DESIGN ASSISTANTS	THOM SWANN, GABRIELLA VOYIAS
READER	CARLA MANFREDINO
CONTRIBUTING EDITORS	JACOB BROMBERG, LAUREN ELKIN, EMMELINE FRANCIS,
	ORIT GAT, PATRICK LANGLEY, BELLA MARRIN, DANIEL MEDIN,
	SAM SOLNICK, EMILY STOKES, KISHANI WIDYARATNA
ADVERTISING	IZABELLA SCOTT
HONORARY TRUSTEES	MICHAEL AMHERST, DEREK ARMSTRONG, HUGUES DE DIVONNE,
	SIMON FAN, NIALL HOBHOUSE, CATARINA LEIGH-PEMBERTON,
	MICHAEL LEUE, TOM MORRISON-BELL, AMY POLLNER,
	CÉCILE DE ROCHEQUAIRIE, EMMANUEL ROMAN,
	HUBERT TESTARD, MICHEL TESTARD, GORDON VENEKLASEN,
	DANIELA & RON WILLSON, CAROLINE YOUNGER

THE WHITE REVIEW IS A REGISTERED CHARITY (NUMBER 1148690)

COVER ART BY NAVINE G. KHAN-DOSSOS
PRINTED BY PUSH, LONDON
PAPER BY ANTALIS MCNAUGHTON (MUNKEN PURE 120GSM, MUNKEN LYNX 150GSM)
BESPOKE PAPER MARBLE BY PAYHEMBURY MARBLE PAPERS
TYPESET IN JOYOUS (BLANCHE)

PUBLISHED BY THE WHITE REVIEW, NOVEMBER 2015
EDITION OF 1,800
ISBN No. 978-0-9927562-6-0

THE WHITE REVIEW, 243 KNIGHTSBRIDGE, LONDON SW7 1DN
WWW.THEWHITEREVIEW.ORG

Supported using public funding by
ARTS COUNCIL
ENGLAND
LOTTERY FUNDED

EDITORIAL

IN *The Art of the Publisher*, Roberto Calasso suggests that publishing is something approaching an art form, whereby 'all books published by a certain publisher could be seen as links in a single chain, or segments in a serpentine progression of books, or fragments in a single book formed by all the books published by that publisher.' A publisher's success can be judged, he continues, by its 'capacity to give form to a plurality of books as though they were the chapters of a single book. All this while taking care – a passionate and obsessive care – over the appearance of every volume, over the way in which it is presented.' With these words Calasso, the legendary director of Italian publishing house Adelphi, captures something of what we attempt with each new issue of *The White Review*, considering it in relation to its predecessors as a new segment in a serpentine progression, or one fragment of a single and as yet incomplete book.

Indeed, in this issue can be seen a continuation of the same themes that have preoccupied us since the beginning of this quixotic publishing venture. New literature in translation – from the extraordinary French novelist Maylis de Kerangal, the great Hungarian László Krasznahorkai and the celebrated Korean poet Ko Un – is complemented by some of the most exciting voices to have emerged from Britain and Ireland over recent years in Caleb Klaces, Declan Ryan and Luke Brown. Our dedication to hybrid, radical forms is apparent in the publication of Anne Carson's 'lyric lecture with chorus' – a work that could as easily be produced on stage or film as within these pages – and Brian Dillon's ekphrastic meditation on charisma, faith, and loss. The combination of art and literature has always been a guiding principle of this project, and here we are delighted to present works by installation artist Alicja Kwade, a photographic series from Germany's Annette Kelm, and new work by Swiss artists Taiyo Onorato & Nico Krebs. Our catholic (a generous interpretation) tastes are reflected in the publication of a long-form essay on a camp in which one comes to terms with one's own death, and another on translation and human subjectivity. Beside this, we are excited to publish interviews with two longstanding heroes of the editors: Zadie Smith, arguably the most important British novelist and critic of her generation, and Rosalind E. Krauss, whose extraordinary body of work over the past forty years dispels the pernicious myth that art criticism must be inscrutable, obscurantist, or anything other than an intellectually and aesthetically exciting experience.

It's a great privilege to be able to present these works to an audience, which is fortunate because Calasso also points out, in case this was ever in doubt, that 'publishing good books has never made anyone terribly rich. Or at least not in comparison with what someone might make supplying the market with mineral water or microchips or buttons.' This we did not need Calasso to discover, though perhaps it is time we diversified into more obviously lucrative sectors (typographically adventurous cat calendars, perhaps, or branded mineral water, formally experimental greetings cards).

In the absence of such a wildly profitable sideline, we are reduced to expressing our thanks yet again to all who make THE WHITE REVIEW possible – its editors, writers, artists, readers, subscribers and, most recently, the supporters of our fundraising campaign. You enable us to continue paying contributors, to put on our unique programme of live readings, screenings, and performances (seventeen in the last year alone, the vast majority of them free to attend), and to provide a platform for new writers. We remain amazed by, and grateful for, the support offered to THE WHITE REVIEW since the first moment of its launch, fifteen fragments ago.

THE EDITORS

MEND THE LIVING

BY

MAYLIS DE KERANGAL

(*tr.* JESSICA MOORE)

THE MARGHERITA SPLATS against the apartment wall and falls to the carpet, leaving the trace of a Neapolitan sunset above the television. The young woman appraises her throw with a satisfied eye and turns back to the pile of white boxes on the counter of the open kitchen, lifts the lid of a second perfectly quadrangular box, slides the burning disc of the Supreme onto her palm, turns to face the wall, elbow bent, hand held as a tray, and with a quick extension of her arm, projects it between the room's two windows, a new action painting, slices of pepperoni drawing a curious constellation on the wall. As she's preparing to break open the third box – a blistering Four Cheese, she banks on the yellowish melted mix being a reliable adhesive paste – a man steps out of the bathroom, glistening, and then – sensing a threat – stops short in the doorway; seeing the young woman wind up for a gesture of propulsion in his direction, he drops to the floor, pure reflex, then rolls from his belly onto his back to observe her from a low angle. She smiles, turns away, eyes scanning her canvas, and taking care to target a new spot, throws the pizza against the front door. Finally she steps over the stunned young man and goes to wash her hands behind the counter. The guy gets up, checks to make sure there are no spots on his clothes, and then takes stock of the damages, turning slowly, a circular scope that brings him back to the woman stationed in front of the sink.

She's drinking a glass of water. Her pearly-white shoulders emerge from an undershirt with the green, white and red of the Squadra Azzurra, the low-cut neck-line hinting at small breasts, free and light; her incredibly long legs extend from a pair of loose blue satiny shorts, and a fine film of sweat pearls above her mouth: she's beautiful as day, maxillaries pulsing beneath the skin of her jaw – fury – and doesn't even look at him as she crosses and uncrosses her long arms of an ancient beauty, low to high, in order to take off her tank top, useless now, revealing a splendid bust composed of various circles – breasts, areolae, nipples, belly, navel, top of the two globes of her buttocks – formed of various triangles pointing towards the ground – isosceles of the sternum, convex of the pubis, and concave of the lower back – crossed by various lines – the dorsal median that emphasises the division of the body into two identical halves, furrow reminiscent of the veining of the leaf and the butterfly's axis of symmetry – all punctuated by a small diamond at the crest of the sternum – the dark hollow at the base of the throat – altogether a collection of perfect forms whose balanced proportion and ideal arrangement he admires, his professional eye valuing the anatomical exploration of the human body above all else, and of this one in particular, delighting in its auscultation, detecting with passion the least disharmony in the elaboration, the smallest flaw, the tiniest discrepancy, the twist of scoliosis above the lumbar vertebrae, this spore of a beauty mark under the armpit, these calluses between the toes at the place where the foot is compressed inside the point of the high-heeled shoe, and the light strabismus of the eyes, coquetterie in one eye when she's lacking sleep, which gives her this distracted look, this air of a girl on the loose that he likes so much.

She pulls on a turtleneck, takes off her shorts to slide into a pair of skinny jeans, show's over, it seems, then puts on high-heeled boots and heads for the door that drips with grease, opens and slams it behind her without a single look back at the young man standing in the middle of the sullied apartment, who watches her go, relieved.

You'll be going to Le Havre Hospital to harvest. It's a heart, and it's now. When he heard this phrase from Harfang's mouth, uttered just as he'd been imagining for months, short and curt, Virgilio Breva nearly lost his voice, the combination of joy and disappointment forming a bitter lump in his throat. Sure, he was on call, and although he was excited by his mission, the news couldn't come at a worse time – rare conjunction of two events that were impossible to miss: a France-Italy match and a desirous Rose at home. And he wondered for a long time why Harfang had bothered to call him in person, suspecting a kind of twisted desire to mock him on an historic evening, because Harfang knew he was a soccer fan – Virgilio had long used Sunday morning practices as a legitimate excuse to save himself from the bike excursions – torture, he would murmur, dumbfounded, seeing the swarm of polliwogs set off with their pointy helmets and multicoloured bike shorts, with Harfang at the centre, playing the queen.

Virgilio's in the back of the taxi heading for the Pitié-Salpêtrière, he pulls his fur-lined hood down to his shoulders and gets a hold of himself. He's all stirred up from the tension of the past hour when what he needs is to be in top form, be on top of his game as never before. Because tonight will be a big night, tonight will be *his* night. The quality of the transplant depends upon the quality of the harvest, that's the governing principle, and tonight he's on the frontline.

It's time to pull yourself together, he thinks, interlacing his fingers in their leather gloves, it's time to call it off with this woman, this crazy broad, and to put self-preservation first, even if he has to deprive himself of her in order to do so, of her hyperactive body and the sparkle of her presence. He goes over the past hour with alarm, Rose surprising him at home when he had planned to go out and watch the game with friends, then demanding, sweet but vaguely threatening, that they stay home to watch it together and order pizza, already equipped with a playful point in her favour – this *azzurra* soccer fan outfit; the erotic tension between them coiling gradually with that other tension, war-like and upper case, of the match to come, a madly alluring mix that seeped potential happiness, and Harfang's call at the stroke of 8.oo had pushed things to a fever pitch, the agitation going off the scale, penetrating the roof. He'd leapt to his feet immediately and answered I'm here, I'm ready, I'm on

F

my way, avoiding Rose's eyes but exaggerating a tragic look – eyebrows in circumflex accents and bottom lip pulled up over the top one, oval of the chin lengthened sadly – a look meant to convey disaster, bad luck, bad dice, a look meant for Rose, grimacing for her at this moment, hand fanning the air, guignolesque, a tragedian at the bazaar, while his eyes were radiating exultation – a heart! – she wasn't fooled. He backed off to take a shower, get dressed again in something clean and warm, and when he came out of the bathroom, things were already spiralling out of control. A magnificent and exhausting show, one that, now that he revisits it in slow motion, now that he perceives the logical majesty of it, does nothing but increase Rose's precellence, her incomparable splendour and her fiery temperament, the young woman releasing her fury in sovereign style and maintaining a royal mutism where so many others would have simply wailed. Splat! Splat! Splat! and the more he thinks about it, the more it becomes clear that breaking up with her would be folly, this beauty who is both highly inflammatory and entirely unique – he would never give her up, no matter what anyone said, those who took her for a madwoman, those who took her for 'cray–cray' as they say, with a knowing glance, when really they would have given anything to touch that trapeze of warm skin at the back of her beautiful knee.

She had pushed open the door of the required class at the Pitié–Salpêtrière, beginning of the university year, the series of lectures during clerkship in the form of directed studies in a particular subject: the study of clinical cases. During long sessions, real case studies from the hospital or imagined, question–based scenarios were 're–enacted' for the students so they could practise their bedside manner, learn the movements of auscultation, train themselves to make a diagnosis, identify a pathology, and determine a treatment protocol. These practical sessions, structured around the patient–caregiver duo, took place in front of other students and sometimes required the presence of a larger group, in order to facilitate dialogue between different disciplines – the aim was to counteract a compartmentalisation of medical specialities that cut up the human body into a collection of hermetically sealed knowledge and practices, leaving practitioners incapable of seeing the patient as a whole. But this new pedagogy – founded on simulation – aroused suspicion: the use of fiction in the process of acquiring scientific knowledge, the very idea of a re–enactment in the form of a game – they'd say, you be the doctor, and you be the patient – was enough to make the faculty directors sceptical. And yet they consented, acknowledging that this model combined material of a great richness, including subjectivity and emotion, and gave students a chance to work on that fragile exchange, the patient–doctor dialogue (even if it was falsified and displaced) that they needed to hear and learn to decode. In this role play, it was decided that the students would take on the role of the doctors in order to exercise their future function, and so actors were hired to play the patients.

They showed up after the appearance of a small ad in a weekly magazine for

F

theatre professionals. Most of them were out-of-work actors, beginners full of promise or eternal second fiddles in TV shows, surveyors of commercial spots, doubles, extras, silhouettes, running from casting to casting just to make enough to pay the rent – usually a roommate situation in a neighbourhood in the northeast of Paris, or in a nearby suburb – or changing gears to become coaches for training sessions in sales techniques – door-to-door or elsewhere – and sometimes they even ended up taking part in guinea pig panels where they rented out their bodies, tasters of yoghurt, testers of moisturising cream or anti-lice shampoo, experimenters of diuretic pills.

They were a multitude, they had to be selected. Medical professors who were also practitioners formed a jury – some of them theatre lovers, and they took no pains to hide it. When Rose entered the audition room and walked past the benches wearing platform sneakers, burgundy Adidas leggings, and a metallic sweater in sunset colours, there was a stir – didn't they recognise that body and that face from somewhere? They gave her a list of gestures to perform and words to say in order to become a patient who'd rushed to the gynaecologist after discovering a suspicious lump in her left breast and, during the fifteen minutes that followed, her commitment to the role forced their admiration: she even stretched out topless on the floor of the room – tiles here, too – guiding the student's hand, here, here, it hurts, yeah there; as the scene dragged on some discord ensued (and it's true that the student did exaggerate the length of his palpation, going back and forth from one breast to the other, always starting over, indifferent to the words of the dialogue, deaf to the essential information she was still giving him – among other things, that the pain got worse at the end of her menstrual cycle), until she finally sat up, face flushed, and slapped him soundly. Bravo, mademoiselle! She was congratulated, and hired on the spot.

From the very first days, Rose secretly flaunted the terms of the contract, considering that this job she'd landed as a 'patient' for the duration of the university year would be a kind of training for herself, a chance to up her game, to increase the power of her art. She disdained commonplace pathologies (those she believed to be such), and instead hogged all the madness, hysteria, and melancholia, registers she excelled at – romantic heroine or enigmatic pervert – sometimes taking unexpected bifurcations from the original scenario with a nerve that stunned the psychiatrists and neurologists directing the sessions, and created some confusion among the students (they finally asked her to tone it down just a little); she tried her hand at drowning victims, suicidal patients, bulimics, erotomaniacs, and diabetics, liked doing a limp, a deformation (a case of Breton coxalgia gave rise to an interesting dialogue about consanguinity in the North Finistère – hunchbacks – she was able to mimic the rotation of vertebrae in the ribcage) and anything that required her to distort her body; she had fun playing a pregnant woman with premature contractions, but was less brilliant as a young mother describing the symptoms of a three-month-old infant –

stress pearled on the forehead of the paediatric apprentice; superstitious, she turned down cancers.

And yet, she was never better than that day in December when she had to simulate angina. The renowned cardiologist who directed the session had described the pain to her in these terms: a bear is sitting on your thorax. Rose had widened her almond eyes in awe, a bear? She had to round up childhood emotions, the huge evil-smelling cage with grossly hewn plastic rocks, and the enormous animal, some 500–700 kilos, the triangular muzzle, close-set eyes making it seem short-sighted, rusty fur dusted with sand, and the shouts of the children when it stood up on its back paws, two metres tall at its full height; she thought again of Ceaușescu's hunting scenes in the Carpathian Mountains – the bears rounded up by country folk, lured with buckets of food, emerging from the forest at the edge of the clearing where a wooden cabin was mounted on stilts, moving forward right into the frame of the window behind which a Securitate agent was loading the gun and offering it to the dictator (once the bear was close enough that he couldn't miss) – and, finally, she remembered a scene from GRIZZLY MAN. Rose gathered momentum from the back of the room, walked toward the student who was her partner and then stopped – did she glimpse the animal, then, at the edge of some undergrowth, passing its head between two stalks of bamboo or swaying its hips on all fours, nonchalant, liquorice coat, lazily scratching a stump with its non-retractable claws before turning in her direction and standing up straight like a human? Did she see the cave-dwelling monster emerging from months of hibernation, stretching, warming up the fluids that had stopped inside its body, reactivating the drop of blood in its heart? Did she glimpse it rummaging through supermarket waste bins at twilight, growling with joy beneath an enormous moon? Or was she thinking of a different weight entirely – a man? Abruptly, she fell over backwards – the sound of her body falling caused a stir in the room – and in a convulsive tension, let out a shriek of pain that quickly became a silent gasp, and then she stopped breathing. Her ribcage seemed to flatten and hollow like a basin as her face swelled, slowly turning red, lips pressed tight together and going white, eyes rolling back in her head, while her limbs began to fibrillate as though shot through with an electric current. Such realism was rare, and some people stood up to get a better look, alarmed by the crimson face and the concave abdomen; a figure rushed down the stairs of the lecture hall to Rose's side, knocking over the student who'd begun to drone, imperturbable, through the first lines of his questionnaire, and leaned over to revive her while the eminent cardiologist dashed over in turn, aiming a pen-flashlight at her pupils. Rose frowned an eyebrow, opened one eye, then the other, and sat up energetically, peered at the crowd around her, and for the first time felt the pleasure of being applauded – she bowed flat-backed before the students in the bleachers, her first standing ovation.

The young man who had rushed over, furious to have been duped, reproached her for a lack of restraint in her performance, angina isn't a heart attack, you're getting the two mixed up, it's not the same thing, you should have played it with more delicacy and complexity, you're messing up the exercise. To make sure he's been understood, he lists the symptoms of angina one by one – constrictive chest pain, sensation of being crushed across the span of the chest, of being squeezed in a vice, sometimes with other characteristic pains in the lower jaw, one of the two forearms, or more rarely the back, the throat, but you don't collapse; then he details the symptoms of cardiac arrest – heartbeat shoots up to more than 300 beats per minute, a ventricular fibrillation that causes the breath to stop, which causes a blackout, all in less than a minute – he keeps going, he could enumerate the treatments now, list the medications, the antiplatelet drugs that facilitate blood circulation and trinitrine that relieves pain by dilating the coronary arteries, he's bewitched, doesn't know what he's saying anymore, can't stop talking, tosses out sentences like lassos in order to keep her close to him, soon his heart races to an abnormally high speed, a tachycardia that approaches 200 beats per minute, he's at risk of experiencing the very same ventricular fibrillation that he just described, at risk of fainting, ridiculous, Rose has turned toward him, slow, arrogant as a newborn star, looks him up and down and tells him all smiles that there was a bear sitting on her thorax, if he only knew, and says with a glint in her eye, sure, she'll start over again, as long as he plays the bear, he has the physique and the finesse, I'd bet my life on it.

Virgilio Breva does indeed resemble a bear with his suppleness and slowness, his explosive energy. And yet he's a tall dark blond, stubbly beard and smooth hair tossed back, foaming at his nape, straight nose, fine features of a northern Italian (from Frioul). Otherwise the digitigrade gait of the sardana dancer when he's nearing a quintal, the corpulence of an ex-obese man calibrating him in thickness, in fullness, but without visible excrescence; in other words, without folds and without fat – his is simply a fleshy body, an even layer enwrapping him and growing fine toward the extremities of his arms, at his beautiful hands. An attractive and charismatic colossus, of a considerable stature that matches the eloquence of a warm voice, the enthusiastic though marked-by-excess moods, the bulimic appetite for knowledge and the exceptional capacity for hard work; yet his body has its painful fluctuations, an elasticity that causes him to suffer; it contains its share of shame and haunting – trauma from having been mocked, called chunky, tubby, roly-poly, or simply fat, anger for having been scorned, for having floundered sexually, mistrust of all kinds – and lodges all this self-disgust like a supplication in his stomach. Under constant scrutiny, he spent hours being examined for a speck of dust in his eye, was hydrated extensively for a sunburn, inspected closely for a hoarse voice, torticollis, fatigue:

this body is Virgilio's great torment, his obsession, and his triumph – because now it pleases people, it's undeniable, you should see Rose's eyes roving over it – and those who are thick-skinned, jealous of his success, sneer and say that he became a doctor simply in order to learn to master this body, balance its moods, and tame its metabolism.

Top of the class at the residency in Paris, knocking back years of study rapidly, reducing them to twelve, university *clinicat* and assistantship of surgery included, while most students who chose the same course of study stretched it out over fifteen years – but also, I don't have the means, he likes to say, charming, I'm not an old boy, and he plays up the role of the unknown wop, son of immigrants, illegitimate, the hardworking scholarship student, over the top – as creative with theory as he is pro-digiously gifted in practice, flamboyant and proud, carried forward by an Atlantic ambition and an inexhaustible energy, he gets on a lot of nerves, it's true, and is often misunderstood. His mother, panicked by his success, valuing social above intellectual hierarchies, finally looks at him sideways, asks herself how did he do it, what was he made of, who did he think he was, this kid, while he flew into fits of rage to see her wringing her hands and then drying them on her apron, to hear her say plaintively on the day of his thesis defence that her presence was useless, that she wouldn't understand anything, that it wasn't her place, that she'd rather stay home and cook a feast just for him, these pâtés and these cakes that he loved.

He chose the heart, and then heart surgery. People were surprised, thinking he could have made a fortune examining naevi, injecting hyaluronic acid into frown lines and botox into the curves of cheekbones, reshaping the flabby stomachs of multiparous women, X-raying bodies, developing vaccines in Swiss laboratories, giving conferences in Israel and in the States about nosocomial infections, or becoming a high-end nutritionist. Or that he could have basked in glory by opting for neurosurgery, or even hepatic surgery, specialisations that sparkled in complexity and cutting-edge technology content. But no, he chose the heart. The good old heart. The state-of-the-art heart. The pump that squeaks, that leaks, that gets blocked, that's on the blink. A plumber's job, he likes to say: listen, poke and prod, identify the breakdown, change the parts, repair the machine – all that suits me perfectly, hamming it up, hopping from one foot to the other, he minimises the prestige of the discipline while at the same time allowing all of it to pander to his megalomania.

Virgilio chose the heart in order to exist at the highest level, counting on the organ's sovereign aura to rain glory down upon him, as it did upon the heart surgeons who whipped along hospital corridors, plumbers but also demigods. Because the heart exceeds the heart, he is well aware. Even dethroned – the muscle's movement no longer sufficient to separate the living from the dead – the heart, for Virgilio, is the body's central organ, the site of the most crucial and essential manifestations of life, and its symbolic stratification over centuries remains intact. And even more, as the cutting-edge mechanic and ultrapowerful fantasy operator all rolled into one, Virgilio sees the heart as the linchpin of depictions (paintings and poems) that organise the relation of the human being to the body, to other beings, to Creation, and to the gods; the young surgeon is amazed at the way it's imprinted in language, at its recurrent presence precisely at this magic point of language, always situated at the exact intersection of the literal and the figurative, the muscle and the affect; he takes great delight in metaphors and figures of speech in which it is the analogy of life itself, and he repeats ad infinitum that although it was the first to appear, the heart will also be the last to disappear. One night at the Pitié, sitting in the staff room with the others in front of the huge fresco (painted by interns) – a spectacular entanglement of sexual scenes and surgical acts, a sort of gory orgy, campy and morbid, where a few bigwig faces appear from between enormous asses, breasts and pricks, among them one or two Harfangs, most often portrayed in the act, in obscene poses, doggy style or missionary, scalpel in hand – Virgilio told the story of the death of Joan of Arc with flair, eyes shining like marbles of obsidian, slowly recounting how the captive was brought in a cart from the prison to the Place du Vieux-Marché, the square where crowds had gathered; he described the slim figure in the tunic that had been doused with sulphur so she would burn faster, the pyre too high, the executioner Thérage who climbs up to tie her to the stake – Virgilio, galvanised by the attention of those listening, acts out the scene, tying solid knots in the air – before setting fire to the fagots like a man of experience, the arm that lowers the torch onto the coal and oily wood, the smoke lifting, the screams, Joan's cries before suffocation, and then the scaffolding blazing like a flare, and this heart they discovered intact after the body was burned, red beneath the embers, whole, so that they had to stoke the fire again to finally be rid of it.

Exceptional student, intern extraordinaire, Virgilio confounds the hospital hierarchy and struggles to nestle into groups with shared destinies, professing with equal militance an orthodox anarchism and a scorn for family dynasties, incestuous castes, and biological collusions – and yet, like so many others, he is fascinated by all the Harfangs in the profession, drawn to these heirs, captivated by their reign, their health, their sheer numbers; he's curious about their estates, their tastes and their idioms, their humour and their clay tennis courts, so that being welcomed at their homes, sharing their culture, drinking their wine, complimenting their mothers, sleeping with their sisters – a crude devouring – all of this drives him crazy, and he schemes like a madman to get there, concentrating hard as a snake charmer, then hates himself as soon as he awakes, seeing himself in their sheets, suddenly uncouth, viciously offensive, an uncivilised bear rolling the bottle of Chivas under the bed, ransacking the porcelain from Limoges and the chintz curtains, and he always ends up fleeing from there, forlorn, lost.

His entry into the department of heart surgery at the Pitié–Salpêtrière raises his emotionalism a notch: conscious of his worth, he is immediately suspicious of barnyard rivalries, ignores docile dauphins, and works to get close to Harfang, to approach him intimately, to hear him think, doubt, tremble, to catch the very second of his decision and to perceive him in the momentum of his action; he knows that it's by being near him that he will learn from now on, here and nowhere else.

In the taxi, Virgilio checks the composition of the Italian team on the screen of his *telefonino*, checks that Balotelli is playing, Motta too, yes, that's good, and Pirlo, and we have Buffon, then exchanges predictions and insults with two other clinic directors who'll go out tonight and drink to his health before a giant plasma screen, French men who detest the Italians' defensive game and cheer for a team that's physically underprepared. The vehicle speeds along the length of the Seine that lies flat and smooth as a lane, and as they near the entrance to the hospital, Chevaleret side, he makes an effort to quell his excitement and his torment. Soon he's simply smiling, not responding to the messages from the other two, forgetting about the bets and the one-upmanship. Rose's face reappears, he starts to type her a gallant text – something like: the curve of your eyes encircles my heart – and then changes his mind, the girl is nuts, she's crazy and dangerous, and he can let nothing, tonight, come to disturb his concentration, his self-control, he can let nothing affect the accomplishment of his work.

F

❡ The harvesting teams arrive one after the other starting at 10 o'clock. The ones from Rouen show up in a car, since only an hour's drive separates the CHU from the hospital in Le Havre, while those from Lyon, Strasbourg and Paris will have taken a plane.

Coordinating teams have organised their transportation, called an airline that accepted this Sunday mission, and made sure that the little airport in Octeville-sur-Mer is open at night, formalising all the logistical details. At the Pitié, Virgilio paws at the ground with impatience beside the nurse on duty who is phoning everyone – he doesn't immediately notice the young woman in a white coat who is also standing there, silent, and who pushes herself up from the wall when their gazes meet to come toward him, hello, I'm Alice Harfang, I'm the new intern in the department, I'll be doing the harvesting with you. Virgilio looks hard at her: no white lock grows in a cowlick in the middle of her forehead but there is no doubt she's one of them, and ugly, ageless, with yellow eyes and a nose like an eagle's beak, grandfathered in. A shadow comes over him. The handsome white coat with the fur collar bothers him especially. Not exactly the perfect outfit for slogging in hospitals. She's the kind of girl who rolls up like a tourist and believes money grows on trees, he thinks, irritated. Okay, well I hope at least you're not scared of flying? he asks curtly and then turns away as she replies no, not at all, the nurse on duty holding out a freshly printed map, you can go ahead, the plane is on the tarmac, takeoff's in forty minutes. Virgilio picks up his bag and strides toward the department doors without a look at Alice, who follows close on his heels, then the elevator, the taxi, the highways, and the Bourget airport where they pass jetlagged businessmen in long cashmere overcoats clutching luxury handbags, and soon they can both be seen climbing into a Beechcraft 200 and buckling their seat belts without having exchanged another word.

The weather is fair: only a little wind and no snow, not yet. The pilot, a handsome woman in her thirties with perfectly straight teeth, announces good flying conditions and an estimated journey of forty-five minutes, then disappears into the cockpit. As soon as he is seated, Virgilio plunges into a financial magazine left behind on his seat; Alice turns toward the window and watches Paris become a tapestry of sparkling threads as the little plane gains altitude – the almond shape, the river and the islands, the squares and the main arteries, the bright zones of the boutique neighbourhoods, the dark zones of the projects, the parks, all of it darkening if you let your gaze wander from the heart toward the fringes of the capital, above the bright circle of the ring road; she follows the path of tiny red and yellow dots that flow along invisible streets, silent animation of the earth's crust. And then the Beechcraft rises above a hydrophilic substance and here it is – the celestial night; and probably now, disconnected from Earth like this, projected outside any social cadastre, Virgilio begins to think of her differently, the woman who accompanies him – maybe he begins to find her less re-pellent – is this your first harvesting? he asks. She starts, turns from the window and looks at him: yes, first harvesting, and first transplant. Virgilio closes his magazine and warns her: the first part of the night can be overwhelming, its a multiple-organ harvesting, the kid is 19, we'll probably take everything, the organs, the vessels, the tissues, shoop, we'll scrape out everything – his hand opens and closes in an ultrar-apid contraction of the fist. Alice looks at him – her expression, enigmatic, could just as easily signify 'I'm scared' as 'I'm a Harfang – did you forget already?' – then she brings her chair back up and fastens her seat belt again, as Virgilio, jostled, does the same: they're beginning the descent into Octeville.

The little airport has been opened specially for them, the runway is edged with status lights, the tower lit up at the top; the machine sets itself down, shaken by spasms, the door slides open and the footbridge unfolds, Alice and Virgilio step down on to the tarmac, and from that moment on it's a single movement that carries them forward as though they were on a conveyor belt, a trajectory of a magical unbroken fluidity, crossing a barren exterior (this perimeter of pavement where you can hear the sea), a mobile and cosy interior (the taxi), an icy exterior (the hospital parking lot), and finally an interior where they know the codes (the surgical department).

Thomas Remige waits for them like the master of the house. Handshakes, coffees tossed back, they introduce themselves, connections are made and as always the name Harfang radiates its aura. Thomas lists those who are assembled: each team is a tandem composed of a senior surgeon and an intern, to which are added the anaesthetist, the nurse anaesthetist, the O.R. nurse, the nurse's aid, and himself – thirteen of them altogether, it will be a lot of people inside, in the unassailable citadel, the secret cave accessible only to those who know the multiple pass codes, it's gonna be crammed in there, thinks Thomas.

The O.R. is ready. The scialytic projects a white light onto the operating table, vert-ical, casting no shadow – spots gathered into a circular cluster converge their rays on the body of Simon Limbeau that has just been brought in, in his bed, and he still has this air of animation – they are moved to see him like this. He's placed in the centre of the room – he is the heart of the world. A first circle around him demarcates a sterile zone that the circulating staff cannot cross: nothing can be touched, sullied, or infected – the organs they're preparing to collect here are sacred objects.

In a corner of the room, Cordelia Owl is apprehensive. She's changed her clothes, has left her cellphone in a locker in the changing room, and the fact of being separated from it, no longer feeling the hard shape of the black case against her hip, vibratile and sly as a parasite, makes her shift into another reality, yes, it's here that it happens, she thinks, with her eyes riveted on the boy who is stretched out before her, and I'm here too. Trained in the O.R., she recognises the spaces but has never experienced anything but intense procedures aimed at saving patients, keeping them alive, and she struggles to grasp the reality of the operation that lies ahead, because the young man is already dead, isn't he, and the procedure is aimed at healing people other than him. She has prepared the materials, laid out the tools, and now she quietly repeats to herself the order in which the organs are prepared, murmurs behind her mask: first, the kidneys; second, the liver; third, the lungs; and fourth, the heart; then she begins again, in reverse, recites to herself the steps of the harvesting established according to the length of ischemia the organ will tolerate; in other words, its survival time once blood flow is cut off: first, the heart; second, the lungs; third, the liver; and fourth, the kidneys.

The body is laid out, naked, arms outstretched to leave the ribcage and abdomen clear. It's prepared, shaved, swabbed. Then covered with a sterile surgical drape that marks out a window of skin, a cutaneous perimeter over the thorax and the abdomen.

All right, we're ready to go. The first team present in the O.R., the urologists, gets the ball rolling – they are the ones who open the body, and they will be the ones to close it up again at the end. The two men bustle about, an odd pair, Laurel and Hardy, the long and lean one is the surgeon and the short round one, the intern. It's the former who leans over first and makes an incision – a laparotomy, so a kind of cross is drawn on the abdomen. The body is divided into two distinct areas at the level of the diaphragm: the abdominal area, holding the liver and kidneys, and the thoracic, holding the lungs and the heart. Next they place retractors at the edges of the incision, which are turned by hand to enlarge the opening – it's clear that arm strength is called for, together with meticulous technical skill, and suddenly it's possible to glimpse the manual aspect of the operation, the physical confrontation with the reality of what is required here. The inside of the body, a murky and seeping interior, glows beneath the lamps.

The practitioners will prepare their organs one by one. Rapid and rigorous blades cut around each organ to free it from its attachments and ligaments, from the various envelopes – but nothing is severed yet. The urologists, standing on either side of the table, talk during this sequence, the surgeon using the opportunity to train the intern; he leans over the kidneys, breaks down his movements and describes his technique while the student nods, asks the occasional question.

The Alsatians make their entrance an hour later, two women of the same height and build; the surgeon, a rising star in the relatively select field of hepatic surgery, doesn't utter a single word, maintaining an impassive gaze behind little wire–rimmed glasses and working on her liver with a determination that resembles a battle, totally engaged in this action that seems to find its fullness through its very exertion, through practice, and her teammate doesn't let her eyes leave these hands for a second, hands of an unmatched dexterity.

Thirty-five more minutes pass and then the thoracic surgeons arrive. It's Virgilio's play now, his moment has come. He tells the Alsatians he's ready to make an incision, then cuts along the longitudinal section of the sternum. Unlike the others, he doesn't lean over – he keeps his back straight, head inclined, and arms held out in front of him – a way of keeping his distance from the body. The thorax is open and now Virgilio uncovers the heart, *his* heart, considers its volume, examines the ventricles, the auricles, observes its beautiful contractile movement, and Alice watches him appreciating the organ. The heart is magnificent.

He proceeds with astounding rapidity, quarterback's arm and lace-maker's fingers, dissects the aorta and then, one by one, the vena cava: he isolates the muscle. Alice, facing him on the other side of the operating table, is captivated by what she sees, by the procession around this body, by the sum of actions of which it is the object; as she watches Virgilio's face, she asks herself what it means for him to operate on a dead person, what he feels and what he's thinking and space suddenly pitches around her, as though in this place the separation between the living and the dead didn't exist anymore.

When the dissection is complete, they cannulate. The vessels are pierced with a needle in order to insert tiny tubes that inject a liquid to keep the organs cool. The anaesthetist monitors the donor's haemodynamic state on display screens, it's completely stable, while Cordelia furnishes the practitioners with the right tools, taking care to repeat the name of the compress or the number of the clamps or the blade as she places it in the hollow of the outstretched hand, open, in front of her, gloved in nitrile, and the more she distributes, the more sure her voice grows, the more she has the feeling of finding her place. It's ready now, the cannulation is done, they will be able to clamp the aorta – and all the practitioners in the O.R. identify what they have come to take on the anatomical cartography, pick out the piece that's intended for them.

Can we cross-clamp? Virgilio's voice, loud in the room even though it's stifled by the mask, makes Thomas start. No, wait! He shouts it. All eyes turn toward him, hands go still above the body, arms at right angles, they suspend the operation as the coordinator weaves through to reach the bed and lean close to Simon Limbeau's ear. What he murmurs then, in his most human voice, even though he knows that his words sink into a lethal void, is the promised litany, the names of those who accompany him: he whispers that Sean and Marianne are with him, and Lou, too, and Grammy, he murmurs that Juliette is there – Juliette who knows, now, about Simon, a call from Sean around 10 o'clock after she had left several messages on Marianne's cellphone, each one more distraught, an incomprehensible call, because Simon's father seemed to be erring outside language, unable to formulate a single phrase anymore, only moans, chopped-up syllables, stuttered phonemes, choking sounds, and Juliette understood that there was nothing else to hear, that there were no words, that this was what she had to hear, and answered in a whisper I'm coming, then threw herself into the night, racing toward the Limbeaus' apartment, hurtling down the long hill, no coat, no scarf or anything, an elf in sneakers, keys in one hand, phone in the other, and soon the glassy cold became a burn, she consumed herself in the slope, dismantled figurine who nearly fell several times, she was trying so hard to coordinate her stride, and breathing poorly, not at all the way Simon had taught her to breathe, keeping no semblance of a regular rhythm and forgetting to exhale, the fronts of her tibias aching and her heels burning, her ears heavy as during an airplane landing, and stitches piercing her abdomen, she doubled over but kept running along the narrow sidewalk, scraping her elbow against the high stone wall that lined the curve, she hurtled down this same road that he had climbed for her five months earlier, the same turn in the opposite direction, that day of the 'Ballade des pendus' and the lovers' capsule in red plastic that had lifted them up together, that day, that first day, she ran breathless now, and the cars that passed her as they drove up the hill slowed, catching her in the white rays of their headlights, the dumbstruck drivers continuing to watch her for a long time in their rear-view mirrors, a kid in a T-shirt in the street, at this hour, in this cold, and how panicked she looked! then she came into view of the bay window of the living room, dark, and ran even faster, entered the building, crossing a space barbed with flowerbeds and hedges that seemed to her like a hostile jungle, and she rushed again up the little stairway where she stumbled and fell, the carpet of leaves congealed by the cold forming a skating rink, she scratched her face, her temple and chin covered in mud, then the stairwell, three floors, and when she reached the landing, disfigured as the rest of them, unrecognisable, Sean opened the door before she even rang and took her in his arms, held her tightly, while behind him, in the dark, Marianne stood smoking in her coat near a sleeping Lou, oh Juliette, and then the tears came – then Thomas takes the headphones he has sterilised out of his pocket and puts them in Simon's ears, turns on the MP3 player, track seven, and the last wave forms on the horizon, it rises before the cliffs until it envelops the whole sky, forms and deforms, unfurling the chaos of matter and the perfection of the spiral in its metamorphosis, it scrapes the bottom of the ocean, stirs the sedimentary layers and shakes the alluvium, it uncovers fossils and tips over treasure chests, reveals invertebrates that deepen the thickness of time, these 150-million-year-old shelled ammonites and these beer bottles, these plane carcasses and these handguns, these bones whitened like bark, the sea floor as fascinating as a gigantic depository and an ultrasensitive membrane, a pure biology; it lifts the earth's skin, turns memory over, regenerates the ground where Simon Limbeau lived – the soft cleft of the dune where he shared a plate of fries and ketchup with Juliette, the pine forest where they took shelter during the squall and the bamboo thicket just behind, 40-metre stalks with their Asiatic sway; that day the warm drops had perforated the grey sand and the smells had mixed together, sharp and salty, Juliette's lips were grapefruit coloured that time – until it finally explodes and scatters, the splashes fly about, it's a conflagration and a sparkling, while around the operating table the silence thickens, they wait, gazes meet above the body, toes shuffle, fingers wait it out, but each person allows for this pause at the moment of stopping Simon Limbeau's heart. At the end of the track, Thomas takes the headphones off and goes back to his place. Again: can we clamp?

    – Clamp!

The heart stops beating. The body is slowly purged of its blood, which is replaced by a cooled liquid injected in a strong stream to rinse the organs from the inside, while ice cubes are immediately placed around them – and in that moment Virgilio probably casts a look at Alice Harfang to see if she's about to faint, because the blood that flows out of the body pours into a bin, and the plastic of the receptacle amplifies sounds like an echo chamber, it's really this sound more than the sight that makes an impression: but no, the young woman is there, perfectly stoic, even though her forehead is pale and pearled with sweat, so he turns back to his work, the countdown has begun.

    The thorax then becomes this site of ritual confrontation where heart surgeons and thoracic surgeons battle to gain a little more length in this stump of vein, or to gain a few extra millimetres of pulmonary artery – Virgilio, friendly but tense, finally fumes against the guy in front of him, think you could leave me a little slack, a centimetre or two, is that too much to ask?

Thomas Remige has slipped out of the O.R. to call the different departments where the transplants will take place so he can inform them of the time of the aortic clamping – 11:50 p.m. – a fact that immediately sharpens the timeline of the operation to come – preparation of the recipient, delivery of the organ, transplant. When he comes back, the first harvest is happening in total silence. Virgilio moves on to the ablation of the heart: the two vena cava, the four pulmonary veins, the aorta and the pulmonary artery are severed – impeccable caesuras. The heart is explanted from Simon Limbeau's body. You can see it in the open air now, it's crazy, for a brief moment you can apprehend its mass and its volume, try to perceive its symmetrical form, its double bulge, its beautiful carmine or vermilion colour, try to see the universal pictogram of love, the emblem of the playing card, the T-shirt logo – I ♥ N Y – the sculpted bas-relief from royal tombs and reliquaries, the symbol of Eros the charlatan, the

F

portrayal of Jesus's sacred heart in devotional imagery – the organ held in hand and presented to the world, streaming tears of blood but haloed by a radiant light – or any emoticon indicating the infinite strata of sentimental emotions. Virgilio takes it and plunges it straightaway into a jar full of a translucent liquid, a cardioplegic solution that guarantees a temperature of four degrees Celsius – the organ must be cooled quickly in order to be conserved – and then this is protected in a sterile security pouch, then inside a second pouch, and the whole thing is buried in crushed ice inside a wheeled isothermal crate.

Once the crate is sealed, Virgilio says goodbyes all round, but none of those who encircle Simon Limbeau's body lift their heads, no one bats an eye, except the thoracic surgeon leaning over the lungs who answers in a loud voice you didn't leave me much leeway, eh, asshole, he lets out a staccato laugh, while the champion from Strasbourg prepares to uncover the fragile liver, concentrating like the gymnast before she mounts the beam – for a moment there you expected her to plunge her hands into a bowl of magnesium carbonate and rub her palms together – and while the urologists wait to claim the kidneys.

Alice lingers. She focuses on the scene, looks one by one at each of those who are gathered around the table and the inanimate body that is the stunning centre – Rembrandt's 'The Anatomy Lesson' flashes before her eyes, she remembers that her father, an oncologist with long and twisted nails like talons, had hung a reproduction in the front hall, and often exclaimed as he tapped it with his index finger: there, *that* is the human being! but she was a dreamy child and preferred to see a council of witches rather than the doctors that made up her parentage; she would stand still for long moments before the strange characters spread out beautifully around the cadaver, their clothes of a deep black, the immaculate ruffs on which their learnèd heads rested, the luxury of folds as precious as wafer origami, the lace trimmings and the delicate goatees, in the middle of which there was this pallid body, this mask of mystery, and the slit in the arm through which you could see bones and ligaments, the flesh into which the blade of the man in the black hat plunges, and more than admiring it, she *listened* to the painting, fascinated by the exchange there, and eventually she learned that piercing the peritoneal wall was considered for a long time to be a violation of the sacredness of the body of man, this creature of God, and understood that every form of knowledge contains its aspect of transgression, decided then to 'do medicine', if it can even be said that she had a choice, because after all she was the eldest of four girls, the one her father brought with him to the hospital every Wednesday, the one to whom, on the day of her thirteenth birthday, he gave a professional stethoscope, whispering in her ear: the Harfangs are idiots, little Harfanguette, you'll fuck them all over, all of them.

F

Alice backs away slowly, and all that she sees becomes fixed and illuminated, like a diorama. Suddenly it's no longer an absolute matter that she perceives on the table where the body lies outstretched, a matter that can be used and that is shared out; it's no longer a stopped mechanism that they dissect in order to keep the best parts. It becomes instead a substance of an incredible potentiality: a human body, its power and its end, its human end – and it's this emotion, more than any fountain of blood poured out into a plastic bin, that can finally make her look away. Virgilio's voice is already far away behind her, you coming? What are you doing? Come on! She turns and runs to catch up to him in the corridor.

A specialised vehicle drives them back to the airport. They streak along the surface of the earth, and their eyes accompany the movement of the numbers on the dashboard clock, follow the dancing bars of light that lie down and stand up again, come and go in place of needles on their watches, show up as pixelated shapes on their telephone screens. Then a call, Virgilio's cell lights up. It's Harfang. How is it?
    – It's mint.

They skirt the city to the north and take the road for Fontaine-la-Mallet, passing forms, both compact and imprecise, border neighbourhoods, ghettos planted in the fields behind the city, swarms of suburban houses divided into plots around a ring of pavement, crossing through a forest, still no stars, no flash of an aeroplane or a flying saucer, nothing, the driver blasts along the service road well above the speed limit, he's an experienced driver, used to this type of mission, he looks straight ahead, forearms still and tense, and murmurs into a tiny microphone linked to the latest earpiece, I'm coming, don't fall asleep, I'm coming. The crate is wedged into the trunk and Alice visualises the different hermetic cases that encapsulate the heart, these membranes that protect it, she imagines that it is the motor propelling them through space, like the reactor of a rocket. She turns and lifts one hip to peer over the seat back, makes out the sticker on the side of the crate in the dark, and deciphers, among the information necessary for the traceability of the organ, a peculiar note: Element or Product of the Human Body for Therapeutic Use. And just below, the donor's Cristal number.
    Virgilio leans his head back against the seat, exhales, his eyes drift over Alice's profile, shadow puppet against the window, he's suddenly unsettled by her presence, softens: you okay? The question is unexpected – a guy who's been so unpleasant up until now – the radio propagates Macy Gray's voice singing *shake your booty boys and girls, for the beauty in the world* in a loop, and Alice suddenly wants to cry – an emotion that seizes her from inside, lifts and sways her back and forth – but holds back her tears and grits her teeth as she turns her head: yeah, yeah, I'm great. He pulls his phone out of his pocket then for the umpteenth time, but instead of checking the time,

drums on the buttons, growing increasingly aggravated, it's not loading, he mutters, damn, damn. Alice, emboldened, asks him, something wrong? Virgilio doesn't lift his head to answer her, it's the game, I wanted the score for the game, and without turning his head the driver says coldly it's Italy, 1–0. Virgilio lets out a whoop, makes a fist that he lifts inside the car, then immediately asks: who scored? The guy puts his indicator on and brakes, a bright intersection lays out a whitish gap before them: Pirlo. Bemused, Alice watches Virgilio rapidly composing one or two victory texts as he murmurs, that's great, then he lifts an eyebrow in her direction, fantastic player that Pirlo! his smile overwhelms his face, and here already is the airport, the roar of the sea right there at the bottom of the cliff, and the crate they roll along the tarmac to the steps and hoist into the cabin, this matryoshka crate that holds the transparent plastic security bag that holds the container that holds the special jar that holds Simon Limbeau's heart – that holds nothing less than life itself – the potential for life, and that, five minutes later, flies off into the air.

F

INTERVIEW

WITH

ZADIE SMITH

ZADIE SMITH'S BIOGRAPHY is one of contemporary writing's fondest and most famous
yarns of precocious and meteoric literary success. As a student at Cambridge she writes WHITE
TEETH (2000), an ebullient, epically proportioned novel about multicultural London. It gets
picked up by Hamish Hamilton, and on the strength of eighty manuscript pages a two-book,
six-figure deal is struck before she's even graduated. Rapturous praise and a glut of awards
follow. Millennium hangovers have scarcely subsided and Smith is already being hailed as the
'voice of a "new England"'. It is a perfect literary storm.

   All this would be enough to turn anyone's head, but Smith, very wisely, kept hers down.
Two more novels – THE AUTOGRAPH MAN (2002) and ON BEAUTY (2005) – arrived in quick
succession. She spent the next seven years establishing herself as an essayist and cultural critic
of notable range and sensitivity, writing pieces for the NEW YORKER, the NEW YORK REVIEW OF
BOOKS, the GUARDIAN, THE NEW YORK TIMES and the SUNDAY TELEGRAPH – many of which
are collected in the volume CHANGING MY MIND (2009). As a literary critic her roving mind
and resolutely un-buttoned-up enthusiasm for fiction in all its forms have significantly enriched
some of Brit Lit Crit's otherwise tediously dogmatic debates about what novels should be like
and what it is that they do. For a while Smith spoke of herself as a 'recovering novelist', but
before long returned to writing fiction – and to her old stomping ground, Willesden – with her
most recent novel, NW (2012).

   Our conversation took place over email during June and July of this year. When we began,
Smith was busy teaching fiction-writing workshops in Paris, but these days she is generally to
be found in New York, where she has been Professor of Creative Writing at NYU since 2010. In
our correspondence, she reminded me very much of the authorial presence sometimes glimpsed
in her novels: affable, modest and wise. Her responses to my questions were thoughtful and
precise, and ranged widely over topics including the nature of literary innovation, Hollywood
musicals, her move to the US and what lies ahead in her writing.

———

Q. THE WHITE REVIEW — You've written previ-
ously about your teenage love of Hollywood's
Golden Age. Alex-Li, the protagonist of THE
AUTOGRAPH MAN, is also fascinated by the
era, but I wonder whether old Hollywood has
influenced any other aspects of your writing?
A. ZADIE SMITH — The novel I'm writing at
the moment takes that period in Hollywood,
in part, as a subject – but maybe content is a
superficial kind of influence? A lot of writers
have something like it: Chabon and his com-
ics, for example, or more recently Knausgaard
and his bad Eighties rock music. In adoles-
cence your obsessions are formed, and later, if

you become a writer, they will tend to become
'material'. Because this is true I wish I'd devel-
oped cooler obsessions, but what can you do? I
think the more interesting question is the for-
mal influence. And the high artifice of those
pictures, their hyper-reality; I do sometimes
worry that all of that is somewhere deep in the
DNA of what I do. Even if I try quite hard to
construct conventionally 'natural' scenes, 're-
alistic' scenes, I never quite manage it. I was
too saturated by constructed reality as a kid,
and unlike most teenagers (I think) the pho-
nier it was the more I was attracted to it. Those
musicals in which whole European cities or

exotic natural landscapes are reconstructed on Hollywood back lots by Arthur Freed and the like... That was really my childhood mental backdrop whereas, say, Wordsworth (I imagine) grew up with an actual backdrop of trees and rivers.

Q. THE WHITE REVIEW —— As a critic you've been very much engaged in debates about the nature of fiction. You've argued powerfully against some of literary criticism's shibboleths – those to do with what constitutes 'good writing', for example, or the false dichotomy of 'style' versus 'heart' – in favour of a broader and more pluralistic view of what novels are capable of. Do you have any thoughts on why this narrower view of the possibilities of literary narrative continues to dominate amongst certain factions?

A. ZADIE SMITH —— On the one hand everything that's narrow about literary criticism comes from our resistance to the idea of an autonomous literary object, and we resist that idea primarily because novels are made of the same material – words – that we use in our communal, daily, social existence, in the form of speech acts. That's the nub of the problem. We don't sculpt our way through our lives or paint our way through our lives or orchestrate our way through our lives, but we do talk our way through life, and our consequent 'common sense' feeling for language means we often find its 'literary' application stressful in various ways. Tourists will queue all day to see late period Picasso, but not that many people are ever going to read Perec with enjoyment. It's much less important to us that an art object have 'heart' than a novel have 'heart', because we've already cordoned the art object off from our daily life; we take it to be a thing fundamentally separate from us and before which we are required to take on a certain

formal attitude. But when we're put in front of ULYSSES, I think some part of us instinctively rebels. What's Joyce doing with 'our' daily currency? With our everyday words, with the sacred terms with which we baptise our children, or the cooing familiarities we use to profess love to our mothers? What's he doing with the sensible nouns we use to write our laws?

This is all obvious, but I guess where I may differ from a lot of people who make these kinds of points is that I don't conclude from this that the mainstream literary audience is idiotic or that the aesthetic offence which highly stylised uses of language cause isn't in its own way important or worthy of being taken seriously. I think the common sense and communal aspect of language *does* mean the literary object is not quite like other art objects. In the visual arts there's little point in sitting down, in 2015, and painting a perfect replica of the bowl and fruit in front of you. It has been done to the greatest level of perfection; the movement has to be forward. But in the literary arts innovation is *not only formal or at the level of language*, exactly because the medium itself is impure, social, shared, and fundamentally un-cordon-offable. Because of this, innovation can happen at many different levels in literature, both large and small, and I think all of these innovations deserve some measure of respect, or at least not our outright contempt. To me the potential variety of innovation in literature is precisely the consequence of the formal impurity – and beauty! – of writing itself. Along with what can be done with a sentence there are the innovations of perspective, culture, place, history, character – to name a few. The first time I read about a character even vaguely of my own background, Karim, in THE BUDDHA OF SUBURBIA (1990), I experienced it as a literary innovation of an important kind. A certain kind of simple-minded critic might think Kureishi's a book of 'heart' and not an especially stylistically innovative work (when compared to somebody like Perec), but to feel this you really have to feel *so at home* in the canon – that is, *so at home in what has come before* – that the only innovation you can imagine is a radical departure at the level of form: a rupture, a deconstruction (which is often, anyway, just a repetition of modernism itself). But if you never had a natural home in that literary history, it might feel like literature's long journey through forms – and that journey's supposed exhaustion – are not exactly your journey and not quite your exhaustion. You may just be getting started, in fact. When I look at the explosion of African diaspora novels right now, I think: we're just getting started! There's innovation everywhere. It may not be the familiar Joycean form of innovation, but it's real. This is all to say that when I'm reading a novel, as a critic, I am trying to be sensitive to all the different forms of innovation that are possible within our medium, and not to make these childish distinctions between 'style' and 'heart', where the first is supposedly a matter of high form – of the art object cordoning itself from the stain of the cultural or socio-historical or whatever – and the latter being some lowly, sociological matter of 'content'. The novel is not a pure form, it's an unholy mix of old and new, fresh and stale, unique and shared, experimental and conventional, just like language itself. I like it that way.

Q. THE WHITE REVIEW —— Have you found American literary culture more open in this regard?

A. ZADIE SMITH —— It's less on its knees before modernism, to be sure. And less – at the other end of things – enslaved to tradition. I find everything a little lighter on its feet in America; less of the theorising and less of the heritage industry, a little more freshness all round. On the other hand in England I think the intellectual traditions can feel more rigorous, perhaps because many writers here have a traditionally 'academic' background rather than a creative writing background. I feel I'm generally more likely to have an interesting abstract discussion about writing in London than I am in New York. But these impressions may be totally subjective – more to do with my social circles here and abroad than any fundamental difference between the two places.

Q. THE WHITE REVIEW —— In your 2008 essay 'Two Paths for the Novel' you describe an 'ailing literary culture' dominated by what you call 'lyrical realism'. Have things changed at all since then?

A. ZADIE SMITH —— I think the binary thinking of that essay has been elegantly exploded in variety. Just looking around my desk I wouldn't know where to place, in the terms of that essay, Daniel Kehlmann, Jenny Erpenbeck, Elena Ferrante, Ben Lerner, Ma Jian, Peter Stamm, Michel Faber, Joshua Cohen, Nikita Lalwani, Teju Cole, Katie Kitamura or indeed the latest Joseph O'Neill. Despite the shrinking of our industry some really extraordinary writing is being done, and because many writers now have pseudo-academic jobs by which they live, I suspect one positive consequence of this is that they may feel a little freer than before to write as they like. It's the same freedom poets have always had: the freedom of being irrelevant within the market (when compared to J. K. Rowling, E. L. James, Jamie Oliver and so on). My view on that essay now is, I guess, that polemics are temporal, good for shaking things up at a particular moment, but that they wilt and fade beside the incommensurable reality of individual books. I'd rather read any of the writers mentioned above than ever look at that essay again.

Another thing I feel has changed since 2008 is that the fashionable argument against 'realism' has become a bit simple-minded. The now familiar idea that realism 'is just another literary genre' or that realistic writing is always and everywhere unexamined and unconsidered – a form of philosophical naïvety – is in itself, in my opinion, somewhat over-stated. In fact I think we are rather sophisticated in our understanding of the limits and illusions of language, and that this is again largely due to our familiarity with the literary uses of language in everyday life. When you hear, for example, two girls at a bus stop and one is telling the other a 'story' – 'and she was like... and I was like... and they were like' – the story-telling girl is not doing this because she imagines that with this act of mimesis, with this 'realistic' re-telling, she has fooled her listener into believing that what she is presenting is 'authentic' or an unvarnished truth, in some sense essentially 'real' – no. She is performing a speech act in which both parties understand, at least to some degree, that what is happening is a form of 'performance', a bracketed and partial reality.

The problem with the argument that all realism is naïve is that it assigns to both parties in the literary exchange – the reader and the writer – an almost childlike innocence in the face of literary artifice. I've been guilty of this myself. As if only writing that calls attention to its own constructed and artificial nature can be considered writing-without-illusion. Behind this idea lurks a puritan instinct that I think abhors the mixed and fundamentally impure material we work with: language. Like many writers I definitely have this puritan instinct within me, this dream of a writing that

would be pure form, or pure sound, or purely logical, or purely refer to itself. That would never smuggle values and prejudices through the back door: a language that is clear-eyed, stripped of 'belief', utterly material. But as I get older and keep writing I find this dream, too, to be a kind of illusion, and perhaps just as large an illusion as the dream of perfect Stendhalesque mimesis, that is, of believing your prose could be a pane of glass through which reality is perfectly reflected.

Q. THE WHITE REVIEW —— In the same essay you mention having yourself written in a lyrical realist mode, but your more recent works, particularly *NW*, seem to be a departure from this. What has made you want to tell stories in a different way?

A. ZADIE SMITH —— Each novel has its own demands. The one I'm writing now is in the first person, and uses a very different length of sentence, which for me feels like a bigger departure than any other I may have made in the past. These are the differences that matter to writers but are perhaps imperceptible to the reader; I can't tell. It's my instinct to want to tell stories differently each time, I'd be bored out of my mind otherwise.

Q. THE WHITE REVIEW —— Academics don't tend to fare very well in your novels – is this a conscious thing?

A. ZADIE SMITH —— I think it's a response to a romantic form of disappointment. Before I went to university I really worshipped at the altar of the intellectual, of the academic. After passing through a university as a student – and then working in many others as a teacher – well, naturally you can't maintain the heroic image. Immoral moral philosophers, novel-hating English professors, misogynist gender studies experts, venal economists, literally criminal lawyers – I've met 'em all! But I don't think academics are peculiarly prone to bad faith, of course not. It's just that the contrast between the ideal and the reality is so stark within the academy. In our daily lives the line is more obscure, or maybe it's just easier to hide hypocrisy in civilian life, I don't know.

Q. THE WHITE REVIEW — In an article reflecting upon the writing of *NW* you talk about your gift for dialogue, describing the way that characters speak as 'voices that come from nowhere and live on in our consciousness'. Can you tell us how you go about this aspect of the writing process?

A. ZADIE SMITH — Well, that's exactly the part that has no process. Whereas everything else I have to work on very hard. The dialogue I don't think twice about; I just write it down. I don't think there's anything especially magic about it; it's a musical matter of 'having a good ear'. If I hear something generally I can reproduce it. But I can make a lot of errors, too; I'm told there're a lot of tin-eared fake Americanisms in *ON BEAUTY*, for example. But as far as English people go, and of course Londoners in particular, I feel myself to be generally on safe ground.

Recently I was talking with my husband, Nick, who is a poet primarily, and we realised that though I can imitate most voices and he can't do very many, if we're watching an animated movie or listening to the radio, he can recognise all the voices immediately – 'That's Amy Poehler; that's Tiger Woods' – whereas I can't recognise voices even when I know them very well. I can be watching children's TV, for example, and not realise one of the characters is voiced by my own brother, Ben. Thinking about this, I wondered whether these are fundamental differences in our brains – that Nick can 'recognise input', but can't recreate what he hears, whereas I can't recognise input but can export replicas – and I further wondered if this might be one of the differences between poetry and prose writers? That there might be neurological basis for the difference? Maybe that's all nonsense, but it interested me.

Q. THE WHITE REVIEW — One of the abiding concerns in your fiction seems to be with the way that people attempt to make sense of their lives through different forms of binary thinking – be it religious or scientific fundamentalism, Howard's dogmatic iconoclasm about Rembrandt in *ON BEAUTY* or Alex-Li's Jewish-goyish project in *THE AUTOGRAPH MAN*. In your essay 'Speaking in Tongues' you identify a 'middling spot': withholding judgement, moving between voices, worlds, ideas. Is it fair to say that your fiction writing is concerned with sustaining this 'middling spot'?

A. ZADIE SMITH — Completely fair. Sustaining it despite accusations of relativism, sustaining it through and beyond dogma from the right and left, sustaining it in the face of my own profound attraction to binary thinking. Adam Phillips has a collection of essays out with a title that I feel could have been the title of any of my books: *ONE WAY AND ANOTHER*.

Q. THE WHITE REVIEW — Another of the themes of your writing seems to be the exposure of faux-liberal pieties. You've written both admiringly and critically of the liberal tradition of thought. Do you feel that your novels sit comfortably within this lineage?

A. ZADIE SMITH — I am a liberal – and a humanist. I believe in the possible improvement of at least some aspects of human life. But I have no triumphal feeling in connection with either word. To me they both represent a tenuous form of faith – I don't have the illusion that they are perfectly rational categories. I believe

– *I want to believe* – in people, the same way others want to believe in God. But my belief often falters, is often fundamentally unstable, is often weak. And by the same token, I 'believe' in the novel, in the very prosaic sense that reading novels has had a huge impact on my own life and mind. But it's because I was so formed by novels that I am also wary of them; I know how self-congratulatory they can be and how blind about so many things. I know how stupid – for lack of a better word – both the novel and novelists can be. I'm a sceptical novelist and by extension a sceptical humanist. I give both concepts, in the Forsterian sense, two cheers. When I'm writing novels and thinking about them I'm trying to be very clear in my own mind about their values, about what they promote and what they hide, and just how much cant is involved. But it's not so much an accusation as a further area of interest and study: why *is* it so important to liberals to believe that the novel is a humanising force, that it promotes empathy, that it creates moral subjects and so on? How *can* the novel think this about itself and simultaneously be blind to so much else? It's perhaps a stupid analogy, but when I think of novels and the faith they build around them it reminds me of the creation of America, in which two completely opposing thoughts are able to be thought at the same time: 'all men are born equal' and 'black men are sub-human, and so are women, black and white'. That's a classic case of liberal piety: that it can exist in this completely schizophrenic state, stating two opposing things simultaneously. For me the novel is the product of this liberal mentality, for good and for bad. It is about freedom and also absolutely not about freedom. It is about making moral subjects and also absolutely not about that. I had this sense of its double-dealing nature as a student-reader, but now I am a writer-critic and know writers I see how easily that schizophrenic mindset is created; how faulty and fallible writers are and how little in control of their material, really. They do not write from a place of critique outside of the culture, and they are not priests or judges. They're just scribblers, immersed in the illusions and deceptions of their time.

Q. THE WHITE REVIEW —— Very early on in your career your debut novel *WHITE TEETH* was one of those singled out as part of James Wood's critique of 'hysterical realism'. How affected are you by such appraisals of your work?

A. ZADIE SMITH —— Oh, when I was younger very much. When James wrote that I took it no differently than I would have a comment from one of my professors (and of course it was only a year or so after I'd stopped receiving such comments). I took his piece absolutely to heart, as a girl being reprimanded and corrected by a man who knew what he was talking about. And I think a lot of critics wrote reviews of me in that spirit, with that sense that I was a young girl who could do with some firm advice. I often felt completely crushed by such commentary, as I had in college, too. But then again there's something steely in me, there must be, because all criticism of this kind just sent me back to my desk with renewed determination. With James in particular I felt I didn't disagree with him particularly, but I suppose although I agreed with the diagnosis I wasn't convinced by the cure on offer. I don't think (and nor do I think James thinks) that a critic can shape the author's writing on the page, really; criticism and fiction writing are two, to me, equal but different enterprises. Hysterical realism is a good critical story, and I think it will probably last. But I am often struck these days – above and beyond whatever James or I might think

– by how much *WHITE TEETH* means to read-
ers, especially younger ones as well as readers
living in various cultural margins, and I have
become much prouder of that fact as I've got-
ten older. To write that book at 22 – I realise
now that this wasn't too shabby, considering.
And now, at almost 40, when I read reviews,
though I still feel them profoundly I also feel
a basic competency in front of my computer.
I feel I *do* know something about writing that
can no longer be taken from me, not com-
pletely. So I can be made to feel very small
sometimes, but never quite do I feel like noth-
ing, and that's one great advantage, I guess, of
becoming a woman instead of a girl. Twenty
years of other people's opinions has resulted
in slightly thicker skin.

Q. THE WHITE REVIEW —— Around the time
of the publication of your most recent novel,
NW, you spoke of the writing of it as a re-
sponse to your sense of dissatisfaction about
your status as a 'global, international writer'.
Can you tell us more about this dissatisfaction?
A. ZADIE SMITH —— I should be clear: nothing
makes me happier than the thought that I am
being read in Finland or Ghana or Thailand.
But what I didn't want was to sit down at my
computer with that knowledge in my head and
start thinking: *but who cares, in Finland, about
x, y and z?* Or: *how can this bit of slang ever be
translated?* And so on. I didn't want to end up
writing this featureless fiction, with no real
stickiness or sense of locality. I wanted to sit
in my study and not have any awareness of the
professional part of my life: just to write more
or less freely. In the end, very heavily pregnant
and also teaching, that consciousness was all
too easy to achieve. I went to the library every
day and felt I was writing for my life, writing
to remember indeed that writing is what I do
(not just mothering, not just teaching). Finland

was in the end very far from my thoughts.

Q. THE WHITE REVIEW —— *NW* seems in part
to address the end of an era in British culture:
the final collapse of the social democratic set-
tlement and with it the old certainties about
upward mobility and possibilities of achiev-
ing the 'good life'. Did the desire to respond
to these social changes in any way drive the
writing of the novel?
A. ZADIE SMITH —— Explicitly. That's what the
novel is about, the end of exactly that social
compact. It was in large part directly inspired
by a sentence of Tony Judt's which I must have
read in the *NYRB* – or maybe in one of his
essay books – about Judt feeling himself to
be a representative product of a meritocratic
experiment that began in 1945 and ended, as
a positive project, around 1975. I was born in
1975, and I wanted to add an addendum to that;
I felt that my generation was really the last of
the last. Throughout my childhood (though I
didn't really understand this until much later)
there was a fierce war going on to remove pre-
cisely the safety nets and ladders I was at that
very moment using. I was incredibly lucky to
get through before they all got pulled up. Free
schooling, free healthcare, and then free uni-
versity – coincidentally at the same college
Tony went to: Kings, Cambridge. By the time
WHITE TEETH was published and I looked be-
hind to see if the kids were coming up behind
me it was already mostly finished. *NW* for me
was an expression of my own heartbreak at the
end of one version of England, the one I knew,
and the beginning of another. It could just as
easily be called *GOODBYE TO ALL THAT*.

Q. THE WHITE REVIEW —— In the wake of *NW*
you talked of being content with the idea of
not writing any more novels. Is this still the
case? I guess this is also a roundabout way of

asking: what are you working on or interested in at the moment?

^{A.} ZADIE SMITH —— Not at all! I think I must have been depressed when I said that. No, I'm writing more than I have since I was 22. I'm sure it's a consequence of middle age. I feel this huge new energy and this love – LOVE – of writing. And reading: reading has come back, too. I want to read everything. Maybe one thing children have removed forever is ennui, boredom. I'm never bored anymore; no time. I feel I have a lot of work to do before I have to leave the stage in the permanent sense. Another forty years – an optimistic number; I smoke – is very little in terms of word count. I think writers are always aware of this kind of word-count-versus-life-span mathematics. Another six novels, maybe? Probably not even that many. If you're going to write anything you can really be proud of, it's usually in this middle period, 40–60. And that's all I ever wanted out of this: to feel proud. Other people's opinion either way only goes so far with me. I have to feel myself that I've written something of worth, and that's what I'm always working towards.

Right now I'm writing many film scripts, with Nick, and by myself two novels and a book of essays. The first novel was/is a speculative fiction sort of thing but it has been abandoned until I have both kids in school for more hours. I find it impossible to deal with big structural problems – the kind that sort of novel require – in a piecemeal fashion. I need a long, uninterrupted swathe of time. But the essays are almost done. And the second novel is now almost finished, too, though it was meant just to be something to do while I got depressed about the other one. I'm really enjoying writing it. It's about tap-dancing, blackness and slavery. Perhaps it's sort of like an essay on those things, but with

characters. You can imagine how happy the publishers were when they heard that...

No, actually, that's a cheap joke: I think they *were* happy – at least, they said they were. In fact while I'm on record here I should take the opportunity to say that I've been very fortunate at Penguin. They've let me pursue even the most unpromising projects. I don't think even the tiniest, most independent publisher could have given me more freedom in terms of deadlines, practical support and so on. Tap-dancing, blackness and slavery: coming to a bookshop near you, soon.

JENNIFER HODGSON, JULY 2015

ANNETTE KELM

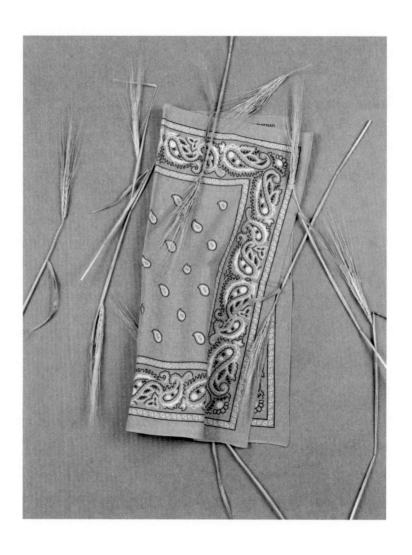

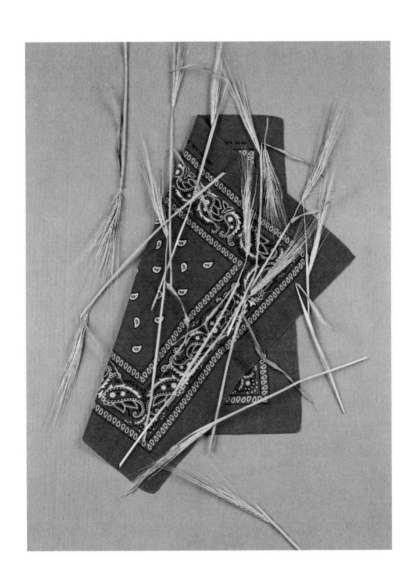

CHARISMA

BY

BRIAN DILLON

THE PICTURE WAS TAKEN by a press photographer some time in the late
1980s or early 1990s. The congregation, hundreds strong at least, has come to a
prayer meeting held in an exhibition hall on the south side of Dublin. They've come
to worship, but also to hope, and some of them are hoping for a miracle, hoping to be
cured. Almost all of them are women in middle age, though very likely younger than
they look, or look to us now, with their complicated hair and complicated glasses.
Dressed as if for church. Imagine what fear and sadness, what so-far-unspoken
troubles they have brought with them on buses out of the suburbs, or train rides from
down the country – stories shared today with strangers, before and after, but held in
the mind now, and offered up, in an anonymous shed where many of them have come
before to stare at *ideal homes* and suchlike.

Sometimes it is hard to comprehend another person's hope, her tremendous
perseverance.

We can assume they're singing and not speaking in tongues, not all of them, not
like this. Their faces compose a selection of mundane ecstasies, such as I know well
from certain churches of my childhood. One of the women is less readable – further
gone, you might say – though familiar in her way.

There are seven or eight hands in the photograph, and six of them are open and
raised, held aloft and aslant in a gesture that seems well known, art-historical even.
But what does it intend, this hand half raised to the ceiling, to the sky? Consider the
woman at bottom left, with the face of a Flemish angel. Her weirdly foreshortened
arm inside its tapered sleeve. Her right hand is raised to heaven but she's not pointing;
she might be in the middle of a blessing, but the disposition of the fingers is all wrong.
(The hand behind her has got it right.) If not a gesture of benediction or deixis – what?
Perhaps it is not meant to *mean* at all, but to receive. It is through their open hands that
something will enter, a gift at last bestowed.

I feel as though I know all of these women well: their bodies, their spirit, their
clothes. I recognise the poise of the woman in white, the way she holds herself together,
there at the centre. I note another's stoic gaze, straight ahead; a third, the youngest, in
the back, with her blurred face on the edge of tears. I look at them and see only, seek
only, one body that I know is not there.

The word 'charisma' derives from the Greek *charis*, which means grace and gives
us the verb *charein*, to rejoice. (If you follow a devious path through Old German and
Old English, you will find that *charein* is related to the verb to yearn, which in turn
may surprise you by signifying in Middle English, and some later Scottish dialects,
both a flowing action and its slow stoppage: congealing or coagulating.) In its most
rigorous theological meaning, *charisma* is first of all a spiritual gift or talent; early
Christians used the word to describe the power of prophecy, the ability to heal the
sick and the tendency to speak in tongues. These are gifts of the Holy Spirit, delivered

as tongues of fire, in a violent ecstatic infusion of the mortal body. In time 'charisma' wandered semantically, but not far at first: before it devolved to its current weak sense of character or personality, the word pointed to a fully supernatural virtue or power. Its historical journey is a little like that undertaken by 'glamour', which once meant a bewitching or spellbinding charm, and now means something more superficial. You can get closer again to the original meanings of *charisma* by noting some related terms, which are less familiar: *charism* and *charismata*.

The Charismatic Renewal is a movement inside the Catholic church that draws on early beliefs in the gifts or *charismata* of the Holy Spirit: healing, prophecy, glossolalia. Charismatics aspire to a direct communication with Christ, unmediated by liturgy. The movement began in the United States, in the mid-1960s, and spread worldwide in the decade following. While traditional Catholics sometimes deplored the Charismatics' turn away from conventional ritual and worship, the Church (the Papacy included) welcomed the renovation in spirituality that they brought, and did not baulk at the boost to church attendance that came with it. Prayer took place in parish churches, in believers' homes, and in meetings or conferences attended by hundreds or thousands of the faithful. Hands were laid on the sick in hope of healing, instances of speaking in tongues were reported, and the ultimate horizon of these meetings was a belief in the real possibility of miracle.

The body and face that I'm searching for – they belong to my mother. It is too late of course; the photograph, it seems, was taken several years after she died. But she had been there: a face in the crowd and a body, perhaps, there at the unseen centre of things: hands laid upon her, voices raised in prayer around her, about her pain and her hope. My mother believed in miracles, she had no choice, but I cannot follow her there – not yet.

(One day I will stop writing about this, rehearsing the bare facts for anyone who will listen, attaching her life and her death to half the things I have to say about books and music and art and stray photographic scraps in which as it happens she had no part. *To write* means: finding reasons to tell you about my mother. One day I will shut the fuck up about her, about my ordinary orphanhood and ordinary grief, cease trying to match her story, her case, to other ideas, other narratives, recondite concepts like *charisma*. I'll stop using these things as excuses – or is it she who's the pretext? – but not yet.)

She had been ill for years, as long as I could remember. At first a vicious, intermittent depression, for which she was tranquillised and prescribed shock therapy: hands upon her already, an ecstasy of shame and fear, the wait to see how much was left of her on the other side. And then, at what might have been mid-life, an obscure diagnosis: the autoimmune disease that would kill her at 50. It was the kind of disease

E

for which all the usual metaphors were horribly real or literalised: this thing seized her, tightened its grip and hardened. Her body became brittle, even air and water hurt her. She turned to prayer – who wouldn't? – and in time fell in with a local group or chapter of the Charismatic Renewal, which thrived in those years among the parish churches of urban and rural Ireland. With a crippled hand she copied out consoling verses from the Bible at her bedside. She exchanged prayers with a countrywide network of the pious and hopeful and desperate; she attended small-scale prayer meetings at the church where we worshipped every Sunday morning, and at last she joined these women, women like them, at mass meetings where, so she later said, the prayed-for person on whom all concentrated their entreaties, their *yearnings*, would sometimes report that a great heat had come into her body, consuming her not with healing force but with hope. I do not believe that my mother ever felt this heat.

If your knowledge or experience of Catholic worship – private prayer being something else – is drawn from centuries of religious art or from the baroque demonstrativeness of the Mediterranean churches, it may be hard to credit just how furtive and shameful public prayer can be for an Irish Catholic. This is what I remember best: bent or buckled figures kneeling before shrines and altars, silently, almost silently, keening their pain into the solid air between them and statue or tabernacle. An ancient voice muttering its penance – for what unthinkable sins? – outside the confessional. And even at mass, hundreds of voices raised to nothing more than a diffident hum, embarrassed before their god and each other. At home we prayed most nights before a muted television, the picture providing just enough distraction, out of the corners of our eyes, from halting, cracked recitations. It was this reserve that the Charismatics had exploded with their frankness of voice and stance and gesture – they felt, and desired, too freely. I am sure this is why I was afraid of them.

When I was 14, maybe 15, my mother took me to the parish prayer meeting, at the monastery to which our church was attached. Who knows why she brought me along. It might have been the frightful state of my own skin: a childhood case of maddening psoriasis, lately joined by the pustular nightmare of bad, really bad, acne. (Some sanctified creep from the prayer group had already, at my mother's invitation, *prayed over my spots* in our sitting room – imagine.) Or perhaps my mother had got wind, amid the vile weather of my teenage moods, of something like her own depression, clouds gathering before her child was even grown. Whatever the reason, one midweek night I sat beside her in a high narrow room among a dozen of the devout, and at length all eyes turned on me, voices too, and hands raised invoking the Holy Spirit. I did not feel: cared for, loved, hoped for, suffused at last with the Spirit. I did feel: a great heat, of a kind.

Middle-aged women of the Charismatic Renewal, you scared this boy half to death. Of course I rebelled against your piety; it was there to be rejected, and it did not belong only to you, it was everywhere. But more than faith and devotion I feared, and then despised, your hope. For where did it get us, and what did it do for her? Nowhere, ladies, and if you'll pardon me, fuck all. Five years of dreaming, panicked, yearning prayer, followed by – what?

Her eyelids flickered around noon, one summer's day in 1985. Had she woken briefly before the end? Had she seen me?

But there's something less bearable than your hope. It's the suspicion that it was here, maybe only here, amid this rapt sorority of the unwell and unhappy, that my mother felt loved. I'm amazed by how you people have let yourselves go, given in together, each alone, to this moment, this atmosphere of expectation, potential deliverance. You there in the overcoat, with your pearls and lapels, your eyes shut and hands out, isolated and embarked on your inner spiritual migration: this frankly does not look like your kind of thing. I've no doubt pain and fear have brought you here just like the others, but something else too: an unthinkable degree of trust. Forget for a moment the prayers, the hymns, the place out of shot where the most stricken are waiting their turn to be blessed. Charismatic women, I do not believe I love you, and it frightens me still to say it, but I think I may have begun to understand you – your insane trust, the ecstasy of your being together like this.

The woman in the pearls looks nothing at all like my mother, who maintained another sort of image in spite of all: suits and gloves and remnants of darkling country-girl glamour. But it is hard not to think, not to ask: when she stood here five or ten years before the photograph was taken, were these her gestures, this the expression, by which she signalled her attention, her readiness, her desire? With her hands extended thus, waiting? In an agony of optimism, waiting and knowing, or suspecting at least, that there was only so much waiting time left. On fire with expectation for another fire, another gift, the gift of charisma.

A WEEKEND WITH
MY OWN DEATH

BY

GABRIELA WIENER

(*tr.* LUCY GREAVES)

We all have tombs from which we travel. To reach mine I have to get a lift with some strangers to a place in the Catalan Coastal Range. I'll be spending the weekend taking part in a workshop called 'Live your Death'. The main challenge of this adventure will be to relate my death in the first person, without really dying, I hope. In the brochure they talk about us facing things very similar to NDEs (near death experiences), watching the film of our lives, glimpsing the light at the end of the tunnel, having out-of-body experiences and seeing languid and distant little men calling us affectionately from the threshold where it all ends. It's also possible, I think, that I'll be put on a plane and taken to an island where weird things happen. In the meantime I'm getting to know some of my fellow passengers.

'Did we meet at "Recycling Ourselves"?' asks the man.

'No, it was at "My Place in the Universe",' she replies.

'Oh yeah... and have you found it?'

'Not yet...'

'After all these workshops you still haven't found it?'

'I'm working on it.'

'What you need is a clear objective,' says the man, who despite all the money he's spent on self-help workshops seems not to have grasped certain basic principles. For example, that you don't greet a woman by asking her if she's figured out what to do with her shitty life yet. I can think of various things to say to them both to solve their problems and earn myself some cash: that he try closing his mouth every now and again and that she tell guys who reckon they know more about her than she does where to go.

'Well, girls, are you ready?' This is the man's second time at the death workshop and he claims to know what he's talking about.

'You have to take your clothes off, yeah? Get naked, yes siree.'

The woman and I look at each other. The man turns around and just speaks to me this time:

'You must have good lungs because you're from over there, down south, people have good lungs there. You're going to need them. I don't want to give too much away, but we're going to grab you by the hair and drown you a bit...'

Even though it's clear he's having us on, the woman, who says her brother persuaded her to come – 'after one of these workshops he left his difficult girlfriend and his horrible job at the bank and became a better person' – is shocked and throws me another pleasantly questioning look.

'Heey, girl, uncross your legs, you'll stop the energy flowing!' says the man.

I do what he says. We're almost there.

E

❡ The workshop centre is a big house in the hills. It's surrounded by trees and has views of the Mediterranean. The huge swimming pool is empty. There are different existential workshops with other groups and topics running at the same time. Emotional education is a luxury item, but some of us can afford it. At reception, next to the herb tea table, I pay the bill and feel a bit dirty, like when you pay for drugs, which is something I don't like doing either. Or when you transfer money to your psychoanalyst.

Paying for spiritual well–being doesn't seem normal to me. Nor does paying for a lung operation, but that's the way things are.

I settle into the small room I'll be sharing with two other people. I put my four changes of comfortable clothes in the wardrobe, my wash bag in the bathroom and, what the hell, I go out to socialise. Apparently one of the aims of the workshop is to find oneself fully with other human beings, something normal people only do after four drinks. A girl sits down next to me.

'"Death"?'

'Yes,' I say. 'You...?'

'I'm in "Death" too. The word already seems a bit less scary, right?'

'Uh... I guess so.' I ask her who the women dressed in white are.

'They're from "Apologise to your Mother". Is it your first time?'

'Yes.'

'Lucky you! It's going to be one of the most important experiences of your life. This is my fourth time.'

People reoffend, and this, depending on how you look at it, could either be a very good or very bad sign. A bell rings and we go into the main room, which has huge windows looking out over the sea. There are more than thirty of us in 'Live your Death' and none of us are wearing shoes. The workshop leader asks us to introduce ourselves and say why we've come. He looks at me and says 'You start', so I have no other choice:

'My name's Gabriela. I'm Peruvian, but I've been living in Barcelona for eight years. I've come because... I'm afraid of death, more so recently, and because I feel disconnected...'

I say all this because it's the truth. There are other truths, but we've been asked to keep it brief.

Before coming, all the participants signed a document in which we promised not to disclose anything that happens here. That's why I've deliberately changed the name of the workshop and I won't use any proper names, not even the workshop leader's, a famous intellectual in Catalonia. I also had to complete a psychological test, one of the ones used to detect your weaknesses. You have to put a series of ideas in order from 1 to 18 and from best to worst. For example, I gave slavery a 15; blowing up an aeroplane

E

full of passengers, a 16; burning a heretic alive, a 17; and torturing someone, an 18.

These are honest answers. I suppose I am a good person, after all.

One by one the others share their reasons, all of which have to do with finding themselves.

The workshop leader explains that this is not therapy. He says it's a time within time. Four days in which we'll experience more than in four months. An experience of dissolving the ego which is, in the end, what death is. A rite of initiation and catharsis to kill the selfish child we all still carry inside, to find our place in a cosmic, social and familial framework. The fear of death is a fear of life.

All that said there's little more to add, except that the workshop entails confronting something as terrifying as 'impermanence'. The idea is that we're going to lovingly discover the greatness of dying and help someone to die, because we'll be expected to play both roles.

In this context, those of us taking part have to find the problems that limit our lives. The technique to achieve this: a kind of consciousness-altering rhythmic breathing in time with music and sounds, all of which will help us to reach a psychic representation of death, heal wounds, and find the cause of our blockages.

Symptoms that indicate the proximity of death and which we'll experience during the workshop while either dying or assisting: dry mouth; dehydration of the skin; use of strange language; the need to return home and reconcile oneself with someone or something; weight loss; feebleness; fragile bones; vomiting; the desire to defecate and expel everything alien to us; death rattles; involuntary movements; glassy eyes.

The workshop is to death what a simulation is to an earthquake. Except, perhaps, for the minor detail that no one will escape death.

Before going to bed we have another task: to draw a self-portrait at tables covered with coloured pencils; I scribble a monstrosity à la Frida Kahlo with a spiny heart and a computer mouse chained to my wrist. Inside my stomach I've drawn a Gabriela with two heads: one is smiling and the other is crying. A typical drawing to impress a psychologist, I think. When I get into bed I start to feel the first effects of the workshop: I can't help remembering the fucking awful bedsores on my grandmother Victoria's body. Bedsores are dead skin, the war wounds of sick people: lying in bed for a decade can be more damaging than battle. Unable to communicate, unable to recognise us, I find it hard to believe she was able to say goodbye or see any kind of beautiful light before she went. I think, too, about the last time I saw my grandmother Elena alive; she had been blind from diabetes for several years, and was on a trolley in the corridor of a public hospital waiting for a bed. She asked me for water, she was really thirsty, so I gave her a sip from a plastic cup. She said: 'I'm going to die, love, take me home, I don't want to die here.' I lied to her: 'You're not going to die, Granny.' I kissed her on the forehead and left. She died an hour later in that same corridor.

E

❡ I haven't been to the doctor for five years. Not even for a miserable check up. Ever since I gave birth I've felt immortal, or I've forced myself to feel immortal. I try only to get ill with things I can cure with a simple visit to the pharmacy. That said, I've been feeling strange for a while now. I don't know how to explain it, I just don't feel well. One day I finally decide to make an appointment with my GP, who in turn books me in with the nurse for a general check-up. He also orders a blood test to see what's going on. I have to wait two weeks for the results. The nurse weighs and measures me and takes my blood pressure. There's nothing wrong with me, of course, doctors have always thought I'm a shambles. It's ridiculous, but every time I leave a consulting room I'm sort of disappointed that I'm not really ill. I don't want to be ill, of course, but for some reason my ego can't handle being so insignificant in any context, even in a hospital. So, when the nurse takes my blood pressure and says 'It's really high,' someone inside me smiles. The devil, perhaps. It's an impulsive, unhealthy delight, revenge for all these years of perfect health. '150/109,' says the nurse. 139/89 is normal.

I'm 35 years old. I'm a woman. In other words, I'm young and up to my eyeballs in progesterone. These two factors are arguably better than a life insurance policy worth a million euros. That's two weighty reasons, I tell myself. 2–0. I win. But it turns out I don't. I haven't got a simple increase in blood pressure because for the whole of the next week I don't eat salt and stuff myself with vegetables and go back to see the nurse and it's 158/110. She takes my blood pressure in my right arm and my left, three times in each. Finally his scientific eminence – my condition merits the presence of the doctor himself – comes out and starts whispering with the nurses.

During these minutes of uncertainty, my blood pressure goes through the roof, 159/115. The doctor says it's not a one-off increase. Nor is it stress, even if I sometimes feel as if I'm going to explode in the middle of everything like a bomb planted by a terrorist who's got the wrong target.

My father found out he had high blood pressure at 35, my current age, and he's taken medication every day since. My grandfather died of a heart attack aged 60; my grandmother Victoria, from a brain haemorrhage. I can't win anymore. The game's turned against me. 3–2. I'm hypertensive. I suffer from stage 1 arterial hypertension. That's all. But hang on a moment, is there any chance the high blood pressure could be a symptom of something worse? How much worse? Something horrible, probably, because the doctor looks at the tip of his shoe. 'The test will tell us,' he concludes. Although we still have to wait for that. Suspense.

Chronic arterial hypertension is called 'the silent plague of the West' and is the principal cause of death in the world, ahead of hunger and cancer and AIDS. It's called this because it acts silently, affecting the blood flow, and is a risk factor for cardiovascular or renal diseases. The cause is unknown in 90 per cent of cases, but almost always has to do with genetics and poor habits. Bingo!

E

No one would say I'm a fat person, but equally no one would say I'm a healthy person. And this is a condition I have borne with pride all this time, which makes me feel alive and lively, the complete opposite of being dead: I drink, I smoke, I go out, I get drunk once a week and once a week I die of a hangover, sometimes I take drugs, I eat junk food, I hate most vegetables, I'm a mother, I'm not baptised, I work in an office, I hate the human race, I'm someone's wife, I stream TV series until three in the morning, I don't exercise, I don't have domestic help, I spend 10 hours a day in front of a screen and the only part of my body that gets any exercise are my fingers hitting the keyboard, like now. It's a miracle my arse isn't the size of Brazil. I'm a journalist who specialises in putting herself in extreme situations and writing in the first person about those experiences. Oh, and I'm almost forgetting the most important thing: I love salt. Coarse-grain salt especially, those tiny diamonds on a good piece of steak, and dips and sauces so salty my eyes roll with excitement. When I was a girl, I remember now, my toxic DNA drove me to sneak surreptitiously into the kitchen when my grandmother Victoria stepped away from the stove and sink my index finger into the red salt pot. Once I'd pulled it off, I'd run with my white, shining finger back to the telly. For a long time, sucking my salty finger while I watched my favourite cartoons was a version of happiness.

¶ Things were beautiful, once. Seriously, they were. Hangovers were generally manageable. And devouring hamburgers and fried chicken had no consequence other than pleasure. I can't say exactly when this impunity ended. It was probably when I turned 30. But I didn't take the hint, I decided to carry on being young and foolish, which goes with the territory of being young, and I kept on living in the only way I knew how, that is: believing I was immortal, never reading the labels on products and publicly declaring myself enemy of the fitness world and its devotees. Only every now and again a glitch in the matrix made me think that something might not be right, a slight acceleration in my pulse rate, for example, as if a savage with a drum had snuck into the magnificent chamber orchestra of my chest.

¶ I touch my face and establish that my spots are still there. I run my hand over my stomach, too, and verify that it's still round, like a four-month pregnancy bump I've grown accustomed to. I stopped worrying about my reflection in shop windows some time ago. I stroke my neck and feel my growing double chin. I think about all this, about the poor fit between my body and the mental image I have of it (in which I prefer the real image not to intervene). It's been a long time I stopped thinking about it, or perhaps I never did.

Back at home, the days following the bad news about my blood pressure are strange. It's no wonder, because I have to start a strict diet in order to become the kind of person I wouldn't bother talking to even if we were stuck in a lift together. I'm not allowed to drink alcohol, maybe a glass of wine or two, but I can't conceive of going to a bar without getting drunk so I stop going out. My girlfriends promise they'll give up lines and gin-and-tonics for me, that they'll switch to spliffs and white wine, but I can tell they're lying. I start to consider a change of friends. Food without salt, on the other hand, is like not eating at all.

The scenario wouldn't be complete without its dose of pharmaceuticals. Every day, for three months to start with, I have to take two five-milligram tablets of Enalapril. The box of sixty costs a disconcerting twenty cents, and the list of possible side eff-ects takes up half the leaflet. Am I supposed to fill my body with these cheap pills for the rest of my life? One day I meet a friend who tells me he has the same condition, that he spends his days eating garlic and doesn't take blood pressure tablets because 'they kill your sex drive'. Hearing this, another close friend says I'd better top myself. Add to this the harassment and takedowns I've been subjected to now that everyone has something to say about my health, especially my family, who once again take the liberty of overprotecting me. I suffer various episodes of anxiety thinking I could have a heart attack at any moment and, as if that wasn't enough, I'm getting my blood pressure measured so often that I've become really popular in the local pharmacies. One night, like every night, I take off my clothes in front of the mirror and see a slight red mark on my right breast, just beside my nipple. I touch it. It's a lump. Something hard. It wasn't there before, I'm sure of that. Then I scream.

∴

LIVE YOUR DEATH DIARY
PART ONE

The first part of this piece is written with the ironic distance I almost always assume because I believe I write better from there. Except now I don't want to do that. It wouldn't be fair to the experience or the workshop leaders or the people who were there giving everything and opening themselves up to others. Nor would it be fair to readers or to myself. I'm going to copy an extract from the diary I wrote that weekend so whoever reads this can see me warts and all:

They've taken our mobiles away, so I don't know what time it is. I'm dead tired. We have to go back in an hour. Today we're breathing. The morning was fun. We danced for two hours, electronica, salsa and a ridiculous song called 'My Tantric Boyfriend'. After that we did contact exercises with partners: looking each other in the eye without talking, touching each other, hitting each other. I was with a really hot, muscly guy, his caresses made me tremble. I liked the exercise where you had to

E

talk non-stop while the other person listened without saying a word. I talked about
my family, about Jaime and Lena. My partner, a young girl this time, was really sad.
She said it made her happy to know I was happy. It made me feel good about my life.
She cried and I couldn't say anything to her because I wasn't allowed to. This is part
of the double experience: repressing the desire to help the other person because in
reality, when the moment comes, no one can help you. We live together, but die alone.

     We spent a long time letting ourselves fall backwards onto a mattress, losing our
fear and, as they say, 'letting ourselves go'.

     What I liked most was the blind person and guide exercise. I was a terrible guide,
I almost killed my partner, who was an older man this time. I made him run and
bump into things so much that he had to sit down and couldn't carry on. When it was
my turn to be blind, my partner was incredibly loving, he took me outside, made me
smell and touch the grass, splash myself with water from the fountain, feel the breeze
and the warmth of the sun. The workshop's probably having an effect, touching my
most sensitive fibres. Every time we do an exercise, somebody cries. After we ate
I saw a boy who lives here playing with two dogs. I remembered that the director
told us to want something badly. That's what I want, more moments in the sun, a
huge garden and dogs that Lena can play with. Strength and patience to bring her
up happily. Are my eyes shining like everyone else's? Have I got a pious smile and
a desire to hug everyone yet? No, I can't be at peace with myself, it doesn't fit my
personality. My position in this workshop isn't the easiest: on the one hand, I feel
I've got to be conscious enough to write this story when I get back, a story about
whether it's possible to try out death, with at least some critical perspective. Because,
let's accept it: you can't try out death, death is a show that goes out live and direct, pure
improvisation. And what does it matter, getting closer to it isn't going to immunise us
against our fear of the void. On the other hand I feel as if thinking like that, with so
little faith, stops me committing to anything, not just to this. I want to try it, I really
want to do it. This workshop is full of dysfunctional, lonely, sad people who feel pain
and don't know where it comes from. Am I superior to them because I don't take
myself seriously or am I the absolute opposite precisely because of that? Am I superior
because I think of myself as happy? I can't carry on kidding myself that other people
are the crazy and dysfunctional ones so as to keep firing witty phrases into the sky.

LIVE YOUR DEATH DIARY
PART TWO

The session finished at almost two in the morning. Today half of us breathed and
tomorrow the other half will have a go. It's my turn tomorrow, so today I was a
carer. The brief is not to intervene in the other person's experience even if we see

them suffering. We can only act if they ask us to. My dying person was a woman of around 40. You have to be patient and humble to be a carer. I spent long hours by her side wetting her lips, holding a plastic bag to collect her sick. The person doing the breathing lies down, their eyes covered. The person caring watches over their deathbed.

We're in a circle, like in a ritual. In fact, the workshop itself is inspired by shamanic sessions with ayahuasca, the famous entheogenic plant. When we were all in position, the music started. The workshop leader guided the session, encouraging us, asking them to be brave to go into the beyond and sometimes playing a drum. The music is key because it makes you travel through different emotional states, from the most violent to the most peaceful. So, in a way, the workshop leader is also a kind of DJ. There was everything from insufferable mystical songs to Wagner's *RIDE OF THE VALKYRIES*. It touched me to hear Mercedes Sosa singing 'I'm bread, I'm peace, I'm more: come on, tell me, tell me all that's happening to you now / because otherwise your soul weeps when it's alone. / We have to get everything out, like in spring. / Look each other in the eye as we speak, get out what we can / so that inside new things grow, grow / grooooow.' The breathing is similar to breathing while in labour: short, rhythmic inhalations and exhalations. Some people breathed sitting down, or even standing until, finally, they reached catharsis. When someone complained about the pain, you could ask the workshop leader to come over and move them. He would press some muscle or other which made the person feel a sharp pain and cry out with relief. I saw people laughing and crying, writhing in pain, shouting as if something had shattered into a thousand pieces inside them, and it's impossible for that not to shake something up inside you. When my dying woman seemed to be at peace, I covered her with a sheet. She had gone.

∴

I've rarely been close to death. Perhaps that's why I'm so afraid of it. For people who see it every day, like funeral directors, death is something ordinary, like sleeping and waking up. My parents always tell the story of when, as a very little girl, I learned that people die. From that day on, whenever they mentioned someone to me, I would ask: 'And have they died yet?' Cue laughter.

Children see death as something strange and fascinating. I don't know at what point death stops being a word in a fairy story and becomes a real circumstance. We spend a large part of our lives thinking of death as something remote and, above all, alien, something that happens to other unfortunate people, until this misleading idea gives way to the painfully physical perception that one day we too will expire irredeemably. Adult life means continually prodding at Nothingness with the fingers of our imagination. This is the bad thing about having precarious beliefs, being pessimistic and vaguely intelligent. More than the instant of death itself, which is already scary enough, humans fear the anonymity of disappearing. Philip Larkin puts it best: 'No rational being / Can fear a thing it will not feel, not seeing / That this is what we fear – no sight, no sound, / No touch or taste or smell, nothing to think with, / Nothing to love or link with, / The anaesthetic from which none come round.'

My first dead person was my grandfather Carlos, the one who had the heart attack. I was 9 years old and my parents told me two days after the funeral. I didn't even see his coffin. I've never gone up to see the body at a requiem mass. I didn't see the bodies of my dogs. I only dared to peek briefly into the room at the funeral parlour where my mother was dressing my grandmother Elena and I saw her foot, dropping to one side in the same comfortable position it used to be in when she was listening to the radio in bed. It was like seeing her alive. I didn't see the body of my grandmother Victoria either because when she finally died I was already in Spain. The only coffin I dared snoop in was my grandfather Máximo's, and only because I hardly knew him.

I've never seen the dead face of anyone I love. This is something else that ranks highly in my list of terrifying things.

I've been scared I'll die countless times, especially on aeroplanes, but only once did I say goodbye to everyone, to my family. A furious wave from the Pacific Ocean tumbled me over on the shore and amidst this whirlpool of foam, with my eyes open, I thought I was going to die, but I came to the surface. During the civil war years in Peru I was more afraid of death than ever. I thought that at any moment a car bomb would blow up in my face or that terrorists and the army would come to our house and cut off our heads. My father's a journalist and I clearly remember the night someone woke him up to tell him eight colleagues had been murdered in a village called Uchuraccay, in Ayacucho. He immediately travelled there and I saw him on TV surrounded by the black bags containing the bodies. I went to the huge funeral procession in Lima and shouted 'justice'. I was 6 years old and that year in Peru was the most violent in its history. Ever since I've had a daughter I'm afraid I'll die of almost anything. In fact I'm so afraid that I don't walk under scaffolding on buildings or cranes lifting cement and I don't cross on red lights. I try to make sure there's not a psychopath behind me on the metro who might want to push me. If a neo-Nazi insults me, I no longer say anything back.

❡ Dinner at our friends' house. Her father is dying of cancer. 'It's hard to be next to someone who's dying, they go from one terrible mood to another in a matter of minutes,' she says. A few days later a friend's mother dies. Another aggressive cancer. My father and his brother, my uncle, both overcame bowel cancer a few years ago. In other words, my genes don't just have the T in hypertension, but also the C for cancer. Not forgetting the D for diabetes. I have the sneaking suspicion that a crow has landed on my tree. 'The white girl,' as they call her in Mexico, must have lost something around here. It's no coincidence that I just killed my sister in a story. And I haven't made a will, I don't have a dying wish and I can't imagine how my life will be without me.

Sometimes I wonder if I'm not externalising my frenzied consumption of five seasons of SIX FEET UNDER. I haven't watched anything else in the last two months and I feel alienated, as if I've put myself in the series or I'm going to die tomorrow. Someone dies at the beginning of every episode; in other words, over the course of five seasons we see some sixty ways to die: from an accident, disease, murder or old age; peacefully, prematurely, violently... In the final episode, flashforwards show us how each of the characters will die in scenes that only last a few seconds and end with their names and dates of death. It's the first time I've thought about the date of the year I'll die. If I live out my whole life and die naturally at an average age, I could die in the year 2050. My grandfather is 93 years old and in perfect health, so if I've been lucky enough to inherit his genes I might stretch it out until 2060. But no longer. I won't see 2070, or 2100. According to the website *thedayofyourdeath.com* I'll die aged 62. 'You have 9,907 days, 00 hours, 14 minutes and 56 seconds left,' it warns me. *Yourfears.com* says I'll commit suicide on 30 December 2040 after losing everything. On *mydeath. com*, it says I'll die in 2024 in a paragliding accident. According to *beingdead.com*, my husband will beat me to death within two years. There are lots of videos on the internet of people talking to themselves and saying how they think they'll die. They're fun. I watch a 20-year-old girl say she's going to die of breast cancer aged 30, and that she's known this since she was a girl, although for the moment she's completely healthy. Death is more here than there.

In SWIMMING IN A SEA OF DEATH, David Rieff writes about the illness and death of his mother, Susan Sontag, and about her deep fear of death after suffering cancer three times throughout her life. He quotes a phrase from her diary: 'Death is unbearable unless you can get beyond the I.' Rieff assures us that, unlike other people, Sontag didn't manage that, partly due to the 'poisoned chalice of hope'. For example, the last poems Bertolt Brecht wrote from his deathbed, says Rieff, discuss the artist's reconciliation with the fact of death, like in the poem where he sees a bird sitting in a tree, whose beautiful song he thinks is even more beautiful knowing that when he dies the bird will still be singing. 'Now I managed to enjoy the song of every blackbird after me too,' he wrote.

Sontag, meanwhile, wounded by mortality, left us this phrase: 'In the valley of sorrow, spread your wings.'

E

¶ My scream startles my husband. Jaime runs to the bedroom and finds me crying with anxiety, clutching my breast.

'It's massive! Why didn't you notice it before?'

'Why didn't *you* notice it before? It's red, can you see?'

'Yes, it's red.'

First thing tomorrow we'll go to the hospital. I look at myself in the mirror again and again. I'm scared to touch it. It wasn't there a few days ago, I would have noticed it. Jaime tells me that if it is a tumour, and we're not sure it is, it'll be treatable. I remember the scene in Rieff's book when he describes how they remove Sontag's breast, an incredibly violent operation which, to get rid of all the diseased cells, has to gouge out a large part of her chest muscle.

I see myself through the looking glass and close my eyes.

I'm tired. It's exhausting being an adult, having to take care of everything and, for that reason, I've often wanted to get ill so people will look after me and I won't have to do anything. I'd be so happy if I could stay in bed watching TV series all the time and sucking liquid food through a straw! I've repeated this dangerous mantra so many times that I ask myself if this unmentionable desire has anything to do with my recent find in the mirror.

That night, unlike others, Jaime and I won't play with the idea of dying, we won't talk about who'll die first, in which ocean we'll scatter the other's ashes and who we'd choose to remarry in case of being widowed. It's not funny anymore. We say nothing and wait for dawn.

¶ Gynaecological emergencies share a waiting room with the labour ward. I watch the husbands pacing and the doctors busy bringing life into the world. At last it's my turn. The nurse asks me to go in alone. I hear a baby cry. The doctor examines me. She feels my breasts: 'I can see it,' she says, 'I can feel it.' I nearly faint.

While she touches my boob I try to cling to something. Something that isn't the word I don't want to pronounce and which, nevertheless, is in the head of every woman having a breast lump checked by a gynaecologist. All I can think about is another book I'm reading at the time, ironically: OTHER LIVES BUT MINE by Emmanuel Carrère, a true story of two events that shocked the author in a few months: the death of a child for her parents and the death of a woman for her children and husband. There I find a reference to the spectacular book MARS by Fritz Zorn, a bestseller that the Swiss writer delivered *in extremis* to his publishers days before dying. In the book he sticks a finger in the wound of the relationship between an insipid life and cancer. The book's opening pulls no punches: 'I'm young and rich and educated, and I'm unhappy, neurotic and alone. I come from one of the best families on the east shore of Lake Zurich, the shore that people call the Gold Coast. My upbringing has been middle–class, and I have been a model of good behaviour all my life... And of course I have cancer. That follows logically enough from what I have just said about myself... [Cancer] is a psychic disorder and I can only regard its onset in an acute physical form as a great stroke of luck.'

Jaime is waiting for me outside. I go out and smile at him. He smiles back. I sit on his knee. I hug him. He hugs me back. We stay like that for a few long minutes. I've only got non–puerperal mastitis (one that doesn't occur when breastfeeding), an inflammatory lesion of the breast.

❡ My tomb is this mattress on which I'm going to travel. My eyes are covered. My carer promises she'll be watching. I breathe deeply, I breathe and I breathe and I breathe, but all I can think about is being there, about the faces of the others. I don't think they like me. Is it possible that I feel like I'm a really nice person but nobody in this workshop realises? The ideas that pop into my head make me think I'm light–years away from being reconciled with myself. Or maybe it's a survival instinct, which won't let me go over to the other side. But I carry on, I try, I breathe increasingly rhythmically. This is hard, when it would be so easy to take LSD or drink a bit of ayahuasca and save ourselves a whole lot of work. The *STAR WARS* theme tune helps me concentrate. It's ridiculous, I know, but it reminds me of Jaime and Lena. I picture them. I hear some of the others shouting, having started their journeys. I feel almost cathartic now. My back starts hurting and I ask the workshop leader to manipulate me. He comes and twists my shoulder blade. The pain is intense. He says in my ear: 'Shout, Gabriela, shout, what would you say to your mother?' I don't know where he got that about my mother, maybe from my drawing or the values test. The only thing I know is that it works. I cry like a little girl, like I did on nights that were too dark, a scream that comes from being alone and afraid: 'Mum, mum, muuuum!' I cry like a wretch. I cry like I haven't done for years. I cry in stereo. I cry so much that I think I've come here to get depressed. I cry and go through all my sad topics. I cry and ask myself if one day I'll be able to stop crying like a little girl. I cry and remember that I'm not the little girl any more, there's another little girl now and I have to look after her. I cry because I'm everyone's daughter: my mother's, my husband's, my daughter's. I cry because I'm scared I'll fail as a mother. I say sorry to my little one for being the infantile person I am. I promise I'll be solid, patient and happy for her. Then I give myself over to the most absolute darkness, I allow it to come, to wrap me as if I'm being embraced by an enormous animal that swallows me and spits out my bones. Now I'm part of its shining pelt. The darkness is warm for the first time, like a black sun; my mind expands inside it. Crying is a way to empty out my contents. I'm empty now, as usual I've cried more than I should have, but I'm not sad because I haven't lost anything. I'm going with everything I am. In the final judgement – this

E

experience tells me – the judge and the accused are the same person. And now I see the beautiful landscape and the blessed light at the end of the tunnel – the cultural fantasy of resurrection and the intuition of mystery – the path to the suspension of all pain, of all fear. I smile to myself. If this is what death is like I don't mind dying tomorrow. I feel someone covering me with a sheet. I've gone.

¶ The good news is that you do come round from this anaesthesia. The following day, in the final meeting where we describe our experiences, the workshop leader suggests an exercise for me: I should go into a corner and write a list of the things that do me good and another of the things that do me harm.

Things that do me harm: being connected to the Internet all day, checking Facebook, bills, KFC, alcohol, drugs, not being with my daughter, my infantilism, the literary world, the pressure of having to write, people's contempt, frivolity, injustice, not being in Lima, salt, not doing exercise, judging others, judging myself.

Things that do me good: sex, Lena's love, Jaime's love, giving love, being loved, cooking, writing, sleeping, going out and seeing the sun, watching TV series with Jaime, laughing, doing absolutely nothing, doing something well, tenderness, not being in Lima, crying, eating healthily without salt.

The survival instinct is moralistic.

It's time to leave the workshop and apply its teachings in daily life. The participants are best friends all of a sudden, they exchange emails, make plans, tell each other about new workshops where they can meet again and carry on trying to find their place in the universe.

It hasn't been one of the most important experiences of my life, as that girl promised, but I feel good, in harmony, so much so that I carry on letting go and head out to walk alone and fulfilled in the countryside; I follow a path that goes into the woods, I walk and walk without looking back, I go a long way without realising and, all of a sudden, I stop still and, looking around me, in the midst of that natural solitude, I become myself again: in other words, I'm afraid an animal will come out and eat me, I remember that I have to go home, to the only place where I feel safe.

¶ I'm getting rid of Lena's nits while she watches TV with her friend Gael. She caught nits at school again. I drag one out with the comb and kill it. Lena is watching ASHA'S INCREDIBLE ADVENTURE. Asha's fish dies in this episode. A friend explains to her that after death there are three possible paths: you disappear, you go to heaven or you're reincarnated.

'What would you come back as?' I ask Lena, but she doesn't answer.

'What would you come back as, Gael? I'd come back as a tree, for example...'

'I'd be a lion.'

'And what about you, Lena?' I press her. 'Go on, say what you'd come back as. A flower? A butterfly? A princess?'

'As me, end of.'

The blood tests showed no problem with cholesterol, kidney function or blood sugar. I'm absolutely fine except for my blood pressure. My diet is pretty boring and I've managed to lose plenty of weight. They'll check my blood pressure again in three months, and if it carries on like it is now, they'll probably increase my dose of Enalapril and I'll keep taking it for life. Beyond that, everything is unpredictable.

I don't know yet where I want my ashes to be scattered. A good place would be in the Nanay river, which goes past Manacamiri, a small village near Iquitos in the Peruvian Amazon, where Jaime and I were really happy. Or perhaps, so as to not suffer from exoticism, in the Mar de Grau, in Lima, where I hope to return one day, or in the Mediterranean, if I don't go back. In the years I've got left, which I hope will be many, I can't write it off, I might find another significant place to spread my wings in this valley of sadness and joy.

On my imaginary headstone, death is still a blank space to be filled. And rain makes the weeds grow.

E

HAIRCUT MAGAZINE

BY

LUKE BROWN

I.

I used to worry about how much more intelligent and successful I would be if I hadn't spent so much time talking to other people, waking up in their homes, never sleeping enough, enraptured by temporary intimacies, by the women I would introduce myself to and the challenges we'd make to each other. What a brighter mind I'd have if I'd stayed in, if I'd read and written much more – and I wished I had behaved differently, until I realised that this was useless, suicidal, that the man I would have become would feel no sympathy whatsoever for the man I am, and I have only narrowly avoided being murdered by him, this superior bastard, this loathsome know-it-all, who would have got away with it completely, and no one would have mourned me. When I think about this I don't feel so bad about my choices.

My name is Paul. I work in a bookshop and write two pages for a style magazine called *HAIRCUT*. The pages were both my idea. I pitched them to the editor – Stev'n, 'rhymes with seven,' he insists – when he was going on dates with my sister and briefly listened to what I had to say. In one page I write about books. In the other I write about haircuts. The juxtaposition of these two pages might perfectly express the contradictions of my soul. I get paid twice the amount to write the haircut page as the books page, and it takes me perhaps less than a tenth of the time. I go out in Hackney and Peckham, approach strangers, and ask if I can take a picture of them to feature in Paul's Haircut Review. Alongside their picture in the magazine and online I award their hairstyle between one and five pairs of scissors – a system I developed personally and which as far as I know is unique. Hair criticism is not a hard science – it is more akin to the interpretation of dreams. Using imaginative empathy like that of an analyst or old-fashioned literary realist, I write a witty summary of what the person attached to the haircut is like, a précis of their secrets and longings, in fifteen to twenty words. Increasingly, I am under pressure from my editor to be cruel. I understand the appeal snarkiness holds to our readers, to our souls. I do my best to resist it. Before I approach the haircut I usually decide how many scissors I am to award and if it's positive I might reveal my rating then and there. I have to consciously fight my attraction to women with fringes, whom I usually award four and a half scissors out of five. Technically, of course, this is nine scissors, but people get confused if you let this sort of pedantry into the equation. I never award five pairs of scissors. Perfect hair is impossible, but the quest for perfect hair provides the page with a sense of telos, something the readers of *HAIRCUT* crave, even if they don't know they do. Hi, my name's Paul and I write for *HAIRCUT MAGAZINE*. I love your hair, it's totally four and a half scissors out of five – would you mind if I put you in the next issue? Often the people I approach giggle and think I am joking. They have been known to sneer and ask me if that is my best chat–up line. But not often. I choose the ones who look friendly.

II.

Contrary to popular stereotype, this is a very friendly city we live in, often heart-breakingly so. Lack of friends is the least of our worries. I can't be the only man who understands that it is just as easy to meet women on public transport as on the internet, particularly if one takes ecstasy before descending into the underground. This fiction that we live in an unfriendly city might have taught us to distrust un-planned encounters with strangers, but the romantic drift of our books and films show we yearn for these meetings too. We don't trust our lack of trust. Our contra-dictions make us imbalanced, tipsy, available. Despite the many tricks of our mobile phones, in tube carriages on a Saturday night there are people on their way to ware-house parties reading D. H. Lawrence, Virginia Woolf, Jean Rhys. East London is full of such intellectual flashers. Whenever I see a Kindle I try to imagine a porn freak, a frotteur. But this is my perversion: the days when reading porn in public was shameful are over, certainly for the commuting women of London. There was a period of a few months when at least 150 shades greyed each train carriage. I would try to gauge from the women's faces whether it was a sexy bit or a plotty bit. I don't mind confessing that this was sometimes a sexy bit of my day. There are very few plotty bits. And there can never be enough sexy bits. Hannah, sister, don't hang your head like that. I am approaching the crux of the issue.

III.

It turns out that a man needs nobler goals in life than mastering the art of introducing himself to women on public transport. Not all men, admittedly, for some men it's enough, men who will lose their looks and charm, end up lonely and embittered. The thing about women is, they'll say, if you don't get away from them in time. If they're lucky they might marry a junior colleague after a campaign of lowering her self-confidence with remarks about her appearance, by buying her drinks, dinner, weeks away, inviting her to move in. Every member of the older generation who owns property holds a purchasing potential over the younger. Perhaps it has always been this way. The young people dream of exacting revenge. Legal documents set out the niceties of the tension. Unlike many of my contemporaries in their thirties I own nothing; my allegiance is with the young, the squatters in this city. These are the people who still talk to me, the ones who live in decaying hospitals and office blocks awaiting destruction. I have walked to their bedrooms through corridors like the scariest level of *RESIDENT EVIL*. It's true, of course, that except for my sweet nature I don't have much to offer my younger friends. Inevitably, they will decide one day that I have been irresponsible with my opportunities, and they will resent me for this.

The last time I saw my sister Hannah she informed me that young men in London are the worst men in the world. This was before the argument really got going; but even then I couldn't miss the accusatory tone. Part of me was proud that she still thought me young, but then I objected to the broad judgement. I hope she will forgive me if I say she's been known to overstate things, to generalise too quickly from particulars. At the very least she might have seen me as an exception. For I have always wanted to be a good feminist. A good man. I don't see any difference beyond the physical between a woman and a man, and I treat women like I wouldn't mind being treated myself, complimenting them incessantly and offering to kiss them. Oh, calm down, Hannah – I'm *joking*. In the basement clubs and mezcal bars, perhaps, in the midnight hour, but not in the bookshop, not in the German supermarket, the exhibition of Chilean pop art. Only in the carnivalesque. The nightbuses. The queues for jerk chicken. The smoking sections. Only very occasionally in the desperate rainy winter mornings. And only after certain glances have been exchanged. If sexism is treating people unequally according to gender, I believe I behave in an exemplary yet heterosexual fashion. But it is of course more difficult than this.

The argument ended badly, with Hannah throwing a glass at my head. That's not quite accurate. Even though she was very angry I'm certain that she intended to throw the glass at the wall *next* to my head. That was four months ago and I have not seen her since.

IV.

We lie to each other all the time about what we think is acceptable from each other. The decline of the institution of marriage has been overstated. It rebranded, became the convenience of sharing property. Nearly everyone in Dalston, a fair sample of the Western world, is united in thinking they think it is OK to have casual sex, but only a small fraction of these people are actual bohemians. Monogamy is never far away. Well, this is natural, I suppose: if you have a nice time you want to have a nice time again. Forever and exclusively until all the niceness has been squeezed entirely dry. And let's be romantic and say that may never happen. In spite of what people said, we quickly realised it was not OK to give people a nice time but not commit to give them a nice time forever, and then the possibility of a shared mortgage. Even the serial seducers knew this. That's what is wrong with the men Hannah mentions, the worst men in the world. They are not principled advocates of polygamy. They believe entirely in monogamy. They like to act like husbands, they like the comfort of the old style. For a night or two at a time, and then they stop answering their phones.

V.

My love life too is completely monogamous, not in fact of course, but in feel; promiscuity will always feel adulterous to me. My Catholic upbringing set too deep. There's very little flavour in what one's allowed to do. I don't even believe in the existence of dates. We're English, we don't date. Dates were created to facilitate episodic narrative structure in American sitcoms – everyone knows this.

Hannah, four years younger than me, is a serial dater, an American from Lancashire. She sees nothing strange about meeting three different men a week, for a date to last forty-five minutes and consist of drinking a coffee. When I go on a date I call it 'going for a drink' and suspect it will continue until last orders, and later, if we're having fun. The risk of this is that in all my new romantic relationships I appear like a man on the verge of falling in love, and make most of my decisions while drunkenly euphoric. This lack of guard is unusual. Even if I were actually in love, and who is to say I am not, I am supposed to remain taciturn at this stage, as though negotiating over the price of a maisonette in Lewisham. I don't preserve the correct distance. I can't ever imagine inferring to a woman sitting across from me that she is one of several I am trying out. I would have to lie not just to her about that but to myself. I don't like the sound of this man at all. So practical; I can hear the ends of his sentences rising like questions, seeking permission for every transactional statement he makes. 'Are you going on a lot of dates at the moment?' 'Quite a few. I want to be certain I find someone compatible?'

'No: I hardly ever go on a date,' is what I say if I am ever asked. And it is almost true, even if I don't mention the women I speak to in Passing Clouds or the Jazz Bar every Friday night, the times I go back to flats with them to drink lager and dab MDMA and listen to 'Let's Dance' as the sun comes up.

I've been living like this for too long. I'm old enough to remember when the sight of heterosexual girls kissing heterosexual girls was brand new. It seemed to happen overnight in the mid-noughties. Earlier in the same-sex schools, probably. Was Katy Perry's 'I Kissed a Girl' symptom or cause? It's for the anthropologists to decide. All I know is everyone was kissing each other, girls and girls then boys and boys. It felt for the briefest of moments like it was enough for everything. We all loved each other. We woke up wrapped in each others' arms and stumbled out to buy breakfast past groups of people looking just like us, right down to the same sunglasses. We probably knew one or two of them intimately and hugged them, breathing in the sweet smell of sweat and sex on their necks, something chemical. Now I wonder sometimes if this city's friendliness is the worst thing about it. There is always someone to inspire new hope in you. There is always a saviour to find.

VI.

When I am not working in the bookshop or reporting on hairstyles I do the work I like the most. This is how I met Emily Franchetti, my favourite writer. It was quite a coup for me and the magazine – she had not consented to an interview in over ten years, and to a photograph in over twelve, and when I wrote to request my interview I had to insist as well on a photograph – most of our readers only look at the pictures. I had never seen her in the flesh before, surprising really, as most of London's writers pass through the shop at one point or other. I don't think I would have missed her, despite there being only the one publicity photo in existence, taken when she was twenty-one and her first novel had just been published. She is what publishers call 'highly promotable' in catalogue copy. Italian good looks. Sharp cheekbones, pouting lips and bright eyes like a 1940s Hollywood starlet. Writers shouldn't look that way. They get enough attention for being just averagely attractive; this was distracting. Particularly for a woman; men, when they're gorgeous, don't suffer in the same way; it's easier for them to be something else too. The photo shows a young woman who knows exactly what the camera is taking from her. She looks straight at it, resentful, about to become furious. She is sick of being looked at like this, sick of what we are trying to claim from her. Her seriousness. Her language. So she scowls and becomes someone who sensitive men want to patronise and cheer up. Someone gallants want to rescue.

It was clear to me there had been a terrible mistake when she agreed to the interview and photo request. While *HAIRCUT* on occasion features some surprisingly good cultural articles, it is also an excuse to print photos of skinny girls in their underwear, often just one piece of their underwear, worn around their ankles. I was terrified about her meeting with the photographer, due round after my interview, a would-be conceptual artist and unrepentant pervert. I hoped he would remember it was a book interview and not try to persuade her to take her clothes off, or pose provocatively on a merry-go-round, or underneath a live swan, or wearing a unicorn horn, or with ice-cream on her face, holding an antique pistol, or a serrated blade to a child's throat, or doing a handstand in a loose dress, on rollerblades, or smoking a Cuban cigar in a wheelbarrow, in a short plaid skirt, wrapped in a butcher's apron covered in gore, or attached to a radiator with cable ties, or joke-shop nails, or actual nails, or any other of his signature moves, but I didn't put it past him. I wished I could hang around to keep an eye on him but I had to work in the shop that afternoon.

VII.

I had not prepared well for the interview. The night before, the magazine had held their Christmas party in a warehouse in Bethnal Green. I would rather have skipped it altogether but it was politic to make an appearance. Jonathan, the advertising sales manager, is a man I studied journalism with at what was then called the London College of Printing: the London College of Placing Your Eggs in the Wrong Backpack. He is a man who I would only cautiously describe as a friend, for reasons I will go into, and last week he had casually mentioned to me that the editor was voicing the possibility of cutting my books page, in favour of a legal highs column.

I had not been reassured by Jonathan's reassurance that, if this did happen, I would be the first choice to write the legal highs column, that Stev'n had a great respect for my ability to enjoy narcotics, and I would probably be paid more money for it. At the party I intended to catch Stev'n when he was flying on a cocktail of empathogens and subtly implant within him an association between my book page and euphoria. But in the end I spent most of the night talking to a woman a few years older than me, the marketing director of a clothing company, about who our favourite character in *MIDDLEMARCH* was – Dorothea, obviously, not the feckless ponce she ends up with – in between accepting bumps of cocaine from the corner of her credit card and downing martinis from the free bar. You wouldn't know from looking at me, but I've got a real thing about novelists from the nineteenth century. I identify strongly with their heroines. Later I heard myself sympathising with the exasperation Charlotte Brontë expressed in her correspondence about her knob of a brother. Both of us, I think, were surprised to be having a conversation about Victorian novels in a crowd of 25-year-olds dancing to rap music, spilling cocktails and taking dabs of MDMA, and it was only a matter of time before Stev'n bullied some interns into kissing each other, and I wondered if the woman I was talking to was sexually interested in me, if she had space in her flat, wanted a child, if we could come to a pleasant arrangement.

I woke up fully clothed with oily hands. The more vivid details of my journey home struggled to arrange themselves into sequence: falling off my bike repeatedly, making emergency repairs, giving all my money to a homeless man after a bin jumped out at me and I rode into a lamppost. I was due at Emily Franchetti's in forty-five minutes. I did not have time to remove the oil from my hands, have a shower or charge my phone – just to pull up the address on my laptop and draw a map on my arm of how to get to her house from the tube stop. I grabbed my voice recorder, splashed some water on my face and ran out of the house, forgetting to take with me the list of questions I had prepared and intended to ask her.

VIII.

Outside her door I took a swig from the small bottle of whisky I had bought at a corner shop. I had felt giddy and happy on the overground; one of the many martinis I had poured into myself must have still been active. When I changed to the underground, however, and started to think about the photographer, I began to feel hot and panicky. I could not work out whether the way the light was flickering in the carriage was a malfunction internal or external to me. I am not a man who usually drinks in the mornings, but it was clear that there was only one solution. The only pubs open at this time are Wetherspoons and I didn't like my chances of finding one in Holland Park.

I was surprised that she lived in Holland Park. The protagonists of her novels are always impoverished women or men, cleaners, waitresses, hotel staff, hairdressers, writers or even less employable artists, all roughly the same age as Franchetti, living in a room of their own, bed, upright chair, no room for books or bag.

The street I was led to by the map on my arm was a quiet, tree–lined curve of tall white–painted buildings. I rang the door bell of one of these elegant structures and waited.

IX.

I was surprised at how friendly she looked, how cheerfully she smiled and held out her hand. More than the intervening years it was the unexpected range of expression that made her look so different to her photograph. Her beauty was still there, but it was warmer and less intimidating when she smiled. Yes, she was only very pretty, terrestrial, made–up with eyeliner, mascara and red lipstick.

I held out my hand and she withdrew hers.

'Oh, shit, yes,' I said.

'Have you been fixing cars?' she asked.

'Tinkering with my Ute,' I said, in an Australian accent. I make bad jokes when I'm nervous. She didn't smile so I reverted to British English. 'A bike, actually.' I looked at my hands. 'It's very hard to get off.'

'The bike?' she asked.

'It was very hard to stay *on* the bike last night.'

She nodded. 'Are you sure you're a journalist?'

'Not really. But I am here to do the interview.'

She weighed me up for a few seconds. 'OK,' she said. 'We're up here.' She had a light Sheffield accent. In a dark blue skirt or dress, a grey jumper and black winter tights, she was wearing no shoes and on the balls of her feet she led me to a set of stairs.

'We're right at the top,' she said, turning back to look at me as if to check what else might be untoward about my appearance. Then she headed up and I followed her.

X.

There is no way I have found or ever attempted of walking upstairs behind a woman without staring at her bum. It was at eye level. I didn't want to look away in case I tripped and accidentally made a grab for it. I wonder if she knew I was looking. She must have had an idea. But what to do with that idea? Stairs are a fact of life. Men are a fact of life. A trudge uphill. Move your legs and get where you're going to.

Aware I might be falling into a trance, I closed my eyes to compose a question, and then I did trip, on the final step, and had to grab her waist so I didn't fall over.

'I'm really sorry,' I said, righting myself.

'It's OK,' she said, but she sounded increasingly wary. 'Perhaps you need a cup of tea?'

F

'I just tripped. Yes, a cup of tea would be lovely.'

I followed her through the door, which opened into a wide wooden-floored hallway with long corridors at right angles from each other. On one side of each corridor fitted bookshelves stretched to the end.

'What was that I saw you swigging through the window?' she asked. 'Brandy?'

'Oh, dear, you saw that. It was whisky, actually.'

'Are you an alcoholic?' She asked this neutrally, as though she'd asked if I came from London. I followed her down the length of a corridor and into what turned out to be a kitchen, shiny, clean, expensive: a piece with the flat.

'No. I'm not yet, anyway. This was untypical, an emergency drink.'

'That sounds like the sort of thing an alcoholic would say.'

'Just a minor alcoholic, though. A major alcoholic would accuse you of being a witch and burst into tears.'

'Are you drunk now?'

'No. Well, a little, enough not to be hungover. Just temporarily deferring future retribution. More or less entirely lucid.'

'Did you consider not getting drunk last night?' she asked calmly, filling the kettle.

'That was my intention. But it was our Christmas party. I did it for literature, actually. I'd planned to buttonhole the editor and convince him of the value of his books page before he replaces it with... I don't know, something typically lurid... a page of weird genitals that look like vegetables, or weird vegetables that look like genitals. Or both. The reader has to guess which is which. I won't share this idea with him. He'd love it. He'd start a YouTube channel. What would they call it? I better not guess. Network TV rights would be sold. It would revive our fortunes. Newspapers would replace their own books pages with versions of it. I could single-handedly bring down book criticism.'

'I'm afraid it might be too late for that already.'

'Maybe. I'm very sorry not to turn up completely sober.'

She took two mugs from a cupboard. 'I'm giving you the benefit of the doubt. There have been times I haven't turned up completely sober too.'

'You're welcome to some whisky, if you'd like.'

'No thanks. Not a whisky girl. Not an anything girl at the moment.'

I nodded, restrained myself from saying, 'Well done.' And when an awkward silence arose, I filled the space with my usual nonsense: 'Do you think hangovers were easier in the past? The great alcoholics got a lot of work done. The kind of hangovers I get might not be conducive to great literature.'

'Well, you probably spend your life throwing coke up your nose,' she correctly surmised. 'I think Scott and Ernest were spared that, at least. And, well, people used to pay them. A lot of the good ones didn't have to do anything else. Quite helpful, a

F

jolt of something at the start of the day or when you're flagging. Something to stop you from getting bored with your own company. And soft drinks are so untasty: they don't have the delicious bitterness of alcohol.'

I looked straight at her, hoping and failing to see a hint of a grin appear.

'I'm sorry if I seem glib about the booze,' I said. 'I suppose I charged in here like a bull in a china shop.'

'You charged in here *sheepishly*. And then you fell over.'

I laughed, and then she smiled, and for the first time I felt like the interview might be something other than a disaster.

'I suppose I'd rather have you than one of the brisk self-loving lifestyle journalists who are bound to show up soon.'

'*Oh*. You're doing other interviews?'

'Yes, for the newspapers, nearer publication. You seem disappointed.'

'No, no. Ludicrously I'd flattered myself that I was the exception to what was still your rule.'

'Desperate times. I've been too aloof. I need to be more realistic. Says my agent. Says my editor. Says my boyfriend. When I agreed to do press for this book I was worried the phone wouldn't ring once. I'm not sure anyone still cares about novels, especially my novels.'

'I met a woman on the bus last year because she was reading one of your novels and I went out with her for nearly a year.'

'From such an inauspicious start, I shouldn't be surprised you're using the past tense.'

'It wasn't all your fault.'

'Which bits weren't?'

'All of it. Except she may have used the fact I liked your books as emblematic of some kind of profundity of spirit that made her think I would treat her kindly.'

XI.

I remembered breaking up with Sophie clearly. I had done it only two months earlier, in a Vietnamese restaurant, at the exact time that someone outside the Vietnamese restaurant had been stealing my bike. I hadn't picked a good place to break up with her. It was as noisy as a school canteen. We were all but sharing a table with the couple next to us, each of whom spoke in the fluent corporate drawl of young people at the start of their careers. We were quieter. Sophie was unemployed. We were eating enormous bowls of Pho. I had overspiced mine with chilli oil and kept coughing in surprise whenever I drank a spoonful. Underneath the glass surface of the table was a town landscape made of straw and I had a childish urge to place small figures there, to arrange an ideal society and imagine myself its leader. We were doing our best not to look at each other, partly because of my portentous behaviour – for days I had not been able to look at her without wanting to wrap my arms around her and take back every cruel word I had not yet said to her – and partly because of the difficulty of eating noodle soup with Western table manners. The restaurant was a truly terrible place to raise the issue of ending a nine-month-long relationship, but this is where we were, and after once attempting to break up with a woman by email, and the resulting fury that had caused, including a dressing down from a complete stranger, you could at least have Skyped her, she hissed, in a supermarket queue, a woman I had never seen before in a supermarket I had never returned to, I knew our culture lacked the respect it had had in the nineteenth century for the written parting letter, knew to do the monstrous thing face to face, to look into Sophie's eyes as I let her know the loving companionship we had enjoyed with each other was at this very moment now over. From one perspective, it was not a big deal. I mean, what was I? Thirty-three years old and nine years older than her, a part-time bookseller, a reviewer of books for *HAIRCUT MAGAZINE*, a man with superficial charm and seven-out-of-ten looks being eroded gradually by a cowardly hairline. I was nothing to cry about. My heart was in the right place, but what good was that to anyone when my brain was in the wrong place, when it had got lost in the corridor and found itself in the girls' toilets again, when it spent too much time in toilet cubicles altogether, when it was like a *VICE* fashion shoot in here? Poor lovely Sophie, far too young for me, impressed by all the fun things about me I think I might want to put away forever.

XII.

But I didn't tell the story in such detail to Emily, with this repellent mixture of guilt and pride. I have flaws *and* friends, being aware of the need to conceal the former. (I tell *you* the unmediated details of my life, my vanished sister, because of our unconditional love and the rich scorn in which you already hold me.) Nevertheless, Emily saw through my presentation – I would have been disappointed if such a gifted writer hadn't, if she'd lacked the arrogance to believe she knew me intimately, generically. It's useful to believe that there are not so many different types of people when you're reaching to understand the secret of another. Even the subtlest portrait-makers select what they see in others according to their own categories, their own capacity of imagination. She must have seen me as self-deluded, vain, messy – her writing enumerated our weaknesses, not to forgive them but to try to avoid them, to eliminate the human. I had a higher tolerance than she did for self-regard, delusion, sweat and lust. Emily wasn't perfect but she looked perfect and her prose was as near as could be. I didn't think she'd ever let me close enough to see the illusions she possessed and where they lay, far below her pale skin. Mine were much closer to the surface, and perhaps that made me more honest than her. But she wasn't bothered about honesty in that sense.

F

She was interested in beautiful form. Her taste was impeccable.

XIII.

'Did you even try to treat her kindly?' said Emily. 'Or do you just feel guilty for dumping her?'

'Did I just use her and then get rid of her and feel bad about it?'

'It sounds like you've reached your own analysis.'

'Probably. I'm sure. Well, I mean – have you managed to treat people kindly?'

'The kindest thing we can do to people is keep our head down as we walk past them.'

'But I love people.'

'Some of my best friends are people. All the more reason you should leave them alone.'

'It's an interesting solution. I'll consider it.'

'No, you won't.'

'No, I won't, you're right.'

The kettle clicked off and she turned to make two mugs of tea. I stepped out of the kitchen back into the book–lined landing.

'Mind if I look at your books?'

'They're mostly my boyfriend's but yes, feel free. It's mostly art books on this side. All the fiction is round the corner. There's a little room I use to write in which holds the few books that have stuck to me.'

I walked away from her. My footsteps informed Emily of the progress of my intrusion.

The art books had been arranged alphabetically, and I noticed the classical good taste of the contemporary choices. I looked for Hirst, Emin, Lucas, the Chapmans – no. Round the corner the fiction began, enough to resemble a second–hand bookshop, too catholic to derive a sense of taste. Whoever she lived with was a big reader with enough space to have as many books as he liked. Judging from the amount of white Picador spines he had done a lot of this reading when I was still a child. I carried on down the corridor, attracted by the light I could see from the room at the end. It was a long room, with two sets of big windows filling it with light and showing the top branches of the tree outside. The walls were covered in paintings, there was a dining table at one side of it, and a living room area formed by two dark red sofas in an L–shape. Hardbacks were piled in a stack in one corner of the room with spines I recognised as recent arrivals to the shop. There was a photo of a middle–aged woman on the mantelpiece, the sort of woman who belonged in this room. I wondered how much the flat had cost when whoever had bought it bought it. I wondered how much it cost now. A pair of black Chelsea boots faced the corner like a dunce.

F

'Sugar?' shouted Emily from the kitchen.

I walked back and said no thanks.

'Your boyfriend, he's a big reader too.'

'When he can. He works hard. Goes to a lot of openings in the evening. I couldn't bear it but he likes it. He's friendlier than me. A lot of the books are actually his ex's. She was in the business until – well, that's his business. I've always been too peripatetic to keep hold of my books. I end up buying the same favourites four or five times.'

'I wouldn't be in a rush to leave here. It's beautiful.'

'It's Andrew's, of course. Like you say . . .' She sighed, and I wondered if it was from relief or guilt or envy or anxiety or simple possession-fatigue. 'I've never lived anywhere a fraction as nice. Sorry – I sound like Daisy Buchanan. "It makes me sad because I've never seen such beautiful shelves before."'

The only Gatsby line that occurred to me to bat back at her was Daisy suggesting that the best thing a girl could be in this world was a beautiful little fool. I restrained myself. That had been my ambition but it hadn't been hers.

'They are nice shelves. What are they, mahogany?'

She looked at me curiously. 'Um, perhaps, yes.'

'It was a wild guess. I know nothing about wood. Or furniture. Just a little bit about books. Which, when you think of it, are sort of made out of wood. Apart from ebooks. Which are made out of Es.'

She laughed at that, a little reluctantly, and shot me a rueful glance. 'I'm sorry. I've never heard that word. What's an ebook?' She kept her face admirably straight and so did I.

'I'm not an expert. But I think I've seen people reading them on the bus on what look like ... etch-a-sketches.'

'Those large ... *calculators* everyone is carrying around these days?'

'Yes. They're reading WAR AND PEACE on them.'

'Middlebrows, everywhere.'

'Books about troubled millionaires who have an addiction to spanking also prove popular.'

'I'm not surprised!' she said, faux-wide-eyed. And in the act of acting she became Hepburn, silverscreen, gorgeous, and I wondered if she had other personalities she showed to other people. Then she handed me a tea. 'Probably easiest to do it in my room.' I was thrown for a second, but she continued. 'The living room's too distracting. You just want to stare out of the window at the swaying branches. I don't allow myself in there when I have work to do.'

She led me back down the corridor and opened a door. The first thing I saw was a double bed and I hoped I might have got it wrong about the boyfriend, that she was only a lodger.

'It was the guest bedroom before I took it over,' she explained. 'Supposed to be for his daughter but she never stays over, not now I'm here.'

She turned sharply away from me as she said that, and I didn't ask any further.

It was a big enough room for a bed, a wardrobe, a neat desk in one corner and a sofa facing it. A white Ikea bookcase, the same type as the three I had crammed into my room, was out of keeping with the display furniture of the corridors, and stuffed full of paperbacks, unalphabetised. Two piles were stacked next to it, jenga towers a couple of moves away from collapsing. She turned the desk chair around to the sofa and gestured for me to sit down there.

'Thanks for agreeing to do the interview,' I said. 'You may have been surprised to find out we even had a books page.'

'I've never seen the magazine.'

'Well, there's no reason why you should have. Perhaps you'd have browsed through a copy waiting in a hairdressers. There are seventy pages of adverts before you reach the contents page. Anyway, I suspect you wouldn't take out a subscription: it's fairly silly.'

'My publicist was keen to emphasise the quality of the books coverage. That *did* make me suspicious.'

'That's nice of her. She would have been stressing the contrast. There's a toxic level of irony in most of the content. Though I don't know if that's the word actually. I don't know if the photos of the models on the toilet are ironic. Or the concentration–camp fashion shoots. It's a tone that seems to assume its readers are so stoned or distracted it needs to jab a pin in their arm every third page, or every third sentence, or every third word.'

'Why do you write for it, then?'

'I try not to think about that. The women this year are always wearing socks. The editor, he likes white socks the best.'

I was aware I was failing to meet her eye. I was embarrassed. Her tone softened.

'Well … I mean I like socks as much as the next girl.'

'Pervert.'

I looked up and she was shaking her head kindly at me.

'Every year there is at least one feature on Aleister Crowley, which I have to write. The owner is a big fan of him. He believes he can do magic.'

'He believes he can do magic or he believes Aleister Crowley can do magic?'

'Both of them. It's connected. That's why he made so much money managing stadium–rock bands in the 1980s. Black magic.'

'I begin to worry where I fit in here.'

'You're my choice. I'm the magazine's gravitas. When I'm not writing my column about haircuts. Stop raising your eyebrows.'

'I find it hard to work out which bits of your life are real and which made up, and whether you know yourself. I was looking at your wrist. Is that a map?'

'It is, yes.' I pulled up my sleeve further and showed her how to get to her house from the tube stop. 'If we end up becoming mates, I could have it done as a tattoo as a souvenir of today.'

'That would be original. You probably have a "bad tatts" section in the magazine.'

'Let's not talk about that. It's three times the length of my book section.'

I put the recorder on the table.

'So, shall we begin? Emily, tell me about your body art.'

POEMS

BY

DECLAN RYAN

& CALEB KLACES

THE RAT

That's all I can remember; only the rat,
from the whole of the day we spent together.
Not the gallery, not stopping off for coffee,
just walking along the river, the rocky strip,
and coming upon the rat.

That's all, is it?

Yes, at this distance from it, that's the only
thing left of the day. It was white
and bloated with water, flat out on a stone
in supplication. I would have stepped
on it if not for a shout from my friend.

That's something at least, not stepping on it.

It is. That's one good thing. I looked down
when she screamed for a second or two
and saw its head thrown back, its teeth
over its jaw. I'm nearly sure I saw veins
under the fur but that may be invention.

That can happen, you can misremember a thing.

You can, an unpleasant thing especially,
it can sour further when it's thought about.
I remember my friend's face, how she was frozen,
pointing but unable to say a word. She saw it
first, the rat. I had been talking to her.

At least she saw it, and stopped you doing worse.

She did and it's lucky that she picked it out,
it was daylight and not easy to spot being light–
coloured, against grey. Already I see how it'll go;

I'm worried the whole summer will eventually
be remembered for that rat. The whole year, even.

It'll be a while before the whole year, surely?

It might, but it could happen. The memory
isn't easy to control. Where I'd want to think
of happier things I've no choice in the matter,
which is why I'm so concerned. A sight like it
can wipe out a thousand smaller, better ones.

You didn't stand on it, at least, that's something.

It is, you're right. I must focus now on that.

P

JANIE'S SONG

Thank you. This is our last song of the evening.
You've been a dream. Some of you might know it,
it's from one of our first records so bear with us,
we haven't played it in a while.
I wrote it for someone; this girl I knew called Janie;
she existed. Janie's a real person. We lived together
for a while once... I was a kid then.
I wasn't ever straight with her,
looking back now. She'd say she couldn't find me.
She'd always want to argue. I used to walk away.

When I think of her it's mornings...
waking up beside her, how her face was,
so close up I couldn't see her
but I knew. Both her eyes closed
and her make-up on, if we'd been drinking.
Or the mirror... standing side by side
my arm around her.
I'd lean down, she was so much shorter,
so I could kiss her on the head...
try to delay her with a coffee. She'd run a bath
for us to sit in, talking; sometimes she let me wash her hair

and then she took off. Moved out here for some reason.
I don't mean it like that. A cousin, or an aunt.
Who knows? She said she'd write.
She didn't. I moved too... she couldn't,
if she wanted to. I miss her.
I suppose what I'm saying... I mean, I think about her,
and there've been others
but no one like her, no one to just sit with.
Listen, Janie, this is a long-shot, but are you here?

INTER ALIA

After nine months it was nine months later. Intimacy, it had turned out, was interrup-
ted by a desire for intimacy. They were forever beginning again with proxy feelings
grasped from further ahead: attractive stand–ins which over time they recognised as
parts of themselves, only for an unexpected touch to break them once more into a new
set of parts, each one desperate to impose its version of the future. Nine months later
when the small body broke away from the body it had grown into to their surprise
the present tense put them back together again. The animal will not be alone. Time
is coated in the animal, which goes on living as long as they go on. It is necessary
to wait for the next word before moving on to the word after that. After which
another in logical sequence forgetful but hurried enough to sound like persistence
itself; a manner of speaking contrived to move at the tempo the baby keeps alive; not
contingent on a particular past and not anticipating a particular future; only moving
away from or towards being present as it continues, until forty two days had gone by,
when the parents of a child are legally obliged to register the name of the child and the
child with a name with the crown. Before the Registrar of Births and Deaths lifted a
sheet of slightly green watermarked paper from a locked drawer and sent it through
a gravely dustless desktop printer to print the baby's name, sex, date of birth, place of
birth (district and sub–district), her own name and jurisdiction and the present date,
then signed the certificate, the baby was — what?

The technology to construct modern skyscrapers existed long before the sky–scraper
became modern, the problem was the number of stairs. Stepping would have replaced
office work as the office workers' chief activity. Once the lift had released time into
tall buildings it made its way into shorter ones, where more important than its
production of time is its ability to render marginalised sections of society publicly
visible. In M&S one morning the lift doors had closed before either of two fathers,
previously and still strangers both to one another and to the use of department store
lifts, could assert control over a bulky pram at the same time as the order in which
they should exit. The lift, with them and their newborns inside their prams inside, was
reascending. It shocked them both, the existence of another baby. Each father and
pram was multiplied several times in the mirrored walls and the illusion appeared to
extend back into the objects being reflected: each baby was repeated in a foreign pram.
One baby broke the tension. It cried. The other baby didn't cry. The crying baby's
father stroked the side of his baby's head, something he had never done before, a
region beside the eye where he felt a circular patch of skin with more give, deep
enough that he thought the word 'divot', not something he would reckon part of his

child unless he happened to stroke her there. With the first touch the baby's arms flew upwards. The other father's hand covered his jeans pocket, finding his keys before his mind had caught up with the hand's fear that the keys might not be in his pocket. The baby continued to cry, almost silently. A tear rose in the corner of its eye and burst down the side of its head. Until now the baby's father had only seen other people's tears run down her face. The way the tear made its glossy point seemed melodramatic, but he was genuinely wounded. He remembered standing above a river where it flowed underground on the outskirts of a city. The river continued under his feet with the clank of the lift. There was a grate over the entrance to the tunnel collecting detritus collected by the river, including a blow-up doll dressed in a sailor's outfit, perpetually drowning. The sight made him laugh in the same way that his baby's apparently desperate cries made him laugh. Both men, as they watched the baby's arms fall slowly down past its head, all the features of which were dragged into its red choking centre, became aware of the floor's movement upwards, as if it was travelling through their feet as well as the air. 'She doesn't like lifts,' the father of the crying baby said to the father of the baby who was not crying, who replied, 'Sorry I thought she was a he.' 'I did too.' 'So did I.' An expression of curiosity rippled across the silently crying baby's face, before it drained into its centre again, this time making noise. In response, and to finish the conversation before it began, two hands found their way through the unnecessary layers of blankets to pick up the baby. The baby's head jerked backwards as if snagged on the pram and her crying deepened to purple. She appeared to be eating each cry. Her head hit her father's jaw. Her toes raked down his chest. He had recently noticed that among more than a few people he is almost always aware of the location of the most attractive person. It is a measure of the size of a room and the number of people inside it. When a room is too large or contains too many people, the awareness breaks with a feeling like pissing in the sea. After the stadium has drained into the street and part of the crowd annexed and sealed by a train carriage, he is aware for the first time in two hours of someone in particular he is not looking at, and of his own eyes. Imagine lying in a pram then kneeling upright against a person's chest. When and where does presence harden out of isolation? Reaching my chest my newborn daughter cries more loudly then quickly seems overwhelmed by fatigue. She leans everything into my shoulder blade and looks sideways with her eyes and mouth wide open. She is either hungry or too full. Her experience is never enough or too much for her. Lying down is vague and watery. Warm erect touch is explosive and too soon. Nothing comes into view. What impresses on her is a lack, overflowing. Flowing over the land as well as under it, as memory overlaps the present, the river also runs away from the tunnel it disappears into. The transparent riverbed curves over the buried iris and pupil. If I try to imagine what it's like in her mind I wake from deep sleep to making love only for it to be finished. I am left with a feeling of alarm crusted with dry pleasure, while a squirting dark room bends around a rhythm. I am old enough to call the imposition a heart, and am reassured by my 'heart' that what I think just happened happened to me. I am anxious that it did: what if I lent someone a tenner? In contrast, I could borrow a fortune from the baby and she would never get herself together in the present tense to ask for it back. The other father smiles and waves at her in a way that is not an attempt to communicate with her. I look in the mirrored wall to see the expression on my baby's face and see my own face attempting a photo shoot expression, which turns into the fake surprise of having to admit to knowing someone you are hoping not to make eye contact with and I am not fooled. The baby has hiccups. They act severely on her chest, drawing it in deeply and offering her ribs, which take on the appearance of gills. The hiccups have the surprising effect of calming. She seems to be resigned to them, the way the struggling of a fish in your hand will give way to an occasional pulse of contrition or resistance or dying. She is a vehicle for something else's movement: nostalgia. That morning before she left the house for the first time without her mother she was fed. Her eyes, her eyelashes still tucked inside, fall to the side of her head as she pulls on a breast. The breast is a warm round part of her body that is strangely removable. Now these hiccups: with each jolt, the memory of sucking the life from a breast flows backwards. Her body is not a safe place to store milk. Some has pooled tidily on my shoulder. A breast's safety is corrupted in her stomach: boiled and squirted downwards. It is odd that intimacy and embarrassment are the options available to choose from. The mulch smell from the baby's nappy might have embarrassed the fathers, but on this occasion they were totally cool with it. The baby's head began once more to knock at her father's collarbone. Her father and mother were always open to their daughter and yet the baby was always trying madly to open them. She was already inside, there was nowhere to go. But she contained something resistant, hard and unaccountable that neither love nor law could control or dissolve. It scared her parents and they were desperate for it not to disappear. What their daughter knew would be lost with the ability to express it. It would be replaced, when she was approved and when she smiled, by all the wonderful things, each with a watermarked certificate, rights and obligations. The floor of the lift rises through the fathers' feet again as it comes to a stop at the level where they entered. A mobility frame rolls in with a glamorous old woman. She presses the button for the ground floor, composes herself in a corner of the lift and holds out her basket of fudge and stockings for a father to gallantly take. She says, 'That baby is cold.' The father wraps his sweaty baby more tightly in its blanket. The baby is turned and slips into the crook of his arm with its legs tight against his chest. The woman peels back the blanket and runs her eyes over the baby's eye. There is an unprecedented mixing and spread of juices with and around a newborn. It is prodigious, unsettling and never enough. You know what it's like,

P

when you want to place your offspring's head entirely in your mouth. The old lady's mouth has a slight quiver. It is very wet and flat, as if both paralysed and galvanised. She wears white and orange powders, an Elizabethan look which makes the yellow nicotine patch on her forearm incongruously contemporary. Juices such as the baby sick on the breast, which is grey with milk and lined with bloody cuts, the spit left by kisses on the grazes the baby's own fingernails have cut into her cheeks, the baby's piss between the electric piano keys, the bubbles which form between the baby's lips, popped by the powdered nose of an old woman. I imagine the outline of a dressing table in years of powder spilled on stiff brown carpet. The baby in the pram rustles and the woman turns towards it. To move closer to one baby would mean moving further away from another. The lift begins to slow. My baby's eyes close. Imagine dark that is busier than light. The warmth between her legs is dissipating and growing louder. She is different from vertical, she senses, and different from hiccups but not different from the heartbeat she is bent around. Her own heartbeat flows inside the slower rhythm. Two rivers run through the same channel. '"You are happy now",' the woman said, repeating what the father had said a moment before to his daughter. He had not been sure whether the words had been spoken. In the old woman's mouth, the sentence was more of a command than a description. If the baby was told it was happy in the present it would in the future become happy. In the old woman's mouth, the sentence was a commentary on the father's use of the same words, in the same order, to mean something different. 'You want everyone in this lift to know that your baby is happy,' the woman seemed to be saying when she repeated the father's sentence, 'so they will approve.' The three adults looked at the baby which was supposed to be happy. It was undeniably true, as far as they could tell: she was happy. The twitching behind closed eyelids only accentuated the stillness of the rest of her trusting, peaceful body. The father replied on behalf of his child, 'She is.' He wanted to sound neither triumphant nor defensive. The woman laughed warmly. '"She is",' she said. The baby's existence was no longer in doubt. The father's legs tingled as a result of the apparent approval of the maternal stranger, or of the smooth movement of the lift. He was vividly aware of where her feet were in relation to his. Some pressurised air was released somewhere as the lift landed. 'I would have had many babies,' the antique woman said, 'but I was never a citizen of this country. By the time I was legal I was old.' She had retrieved her basket of fudge and stockings and rolled through the doors before I realised they were open.

P

EURASIA

BY

TAIYO ONORATO

& NICO KREBS

ВГОР
СЭГ
Н САМБАР, ҮЗҮҮЛЭ
Д, СТИКЕ
ЖААЗ
ЛДА
АХИАЛ
" ОЧИР " төвийн 2 дав

UNCLE HARRY:
A LYRIC LECTURE
WITH CHORUS

BY

ANNE CARSON

SET:

Some tall piles of folded sheets which a person (or two) is shaking out, folding, refolding upstage centre... Comfortable armchair upstage L. Lectern with reading lamp and microphone midstage R. Row of chairs midstage centre.

CAST:

LECTURER

CHORUS: Four seated Gertrude Steins who resemble Picasso's portrait of her. Each holds up a Gertrude Stein mask on a stick that gets snapped up and down (once in unison) when indicated. CHORUS 4 has a voice 'like a beefsteak' as Mabel Dodge said of GS. CHORUS 1, 2, 3 may use lighter pitches.

[enter LECTURER to lectern]

CHORUS 1:

Anyone looking at us sees we are Gertrude Stein

CHORUS 2:

We are a chorus

CHORUS 3:

A chorus of four

CHORUS 4:

Four is better than one

CHORUS 1, 2, 3, 4:

Now to begin

[all snap masks]

LECTURER:

THE VIEW

He was someone surrounded by having his distance very near as Gertrude Stein said of hills.

   First he was not my Uncle Harry but my father's. I was a child when I knew him. He was already old with hair a white haystack and moustache a horizontal wire brush. He had a way of standing with both hands in the front pockets of his pants and both arms braced against a wind always bearing down on the front of him. He

T

had a way of talking sideways over a pipe that stuck straight out the side of his mouth and clacked on his teeth. He was a champion scyther. It was one of the things he had perfected a 360-degree overhead scything technique that amazed all who saw it. All who saw it were not many. Uncle Harry was a kind of hermit.

Now although he never heard of her and might have disagreed with most things she said in her life Uncle Harry was born the same year as Gertrude Stein. I like a view but I prefer to have my back to it said Gertrude Stein. Evenings Uncle Harry would stand in the hay and look down towards the lake for a long time. He stood so still you would call him a person listening except he was deaf. The lake at that hour was like a detail of an old painting with black-green parts and chunks of blue and thick gold. The setting sun burnt a path across it. You might hear a loon call and as its call echoed down the lake all time disappeared into this. Evening held itself. Evening released and it was night. They say there is a moment at life's end when the soul leaves the body. I don't know if it has a sound. Or a sort of duration that is the sound of sound cocking itself.

CHORUS 3, 4:
He was a full one living

CHORUS 2:
Quite an old codger

CHORUS 3, 4:
No he don't want a lodger

CHORUS 2:
Did the family enjoy themselves

CHORUS 1:
I would say so

CHORUS 2, 3, 4:
Can you repeat that

CHORUS 1:
I love a poetical history

[all snap masks]

LECTURER:

THE LONELINESS

Was he lonely. I don't know. Nine months of the year he lived alone on a farm in the north of Ontario. A near town was five miles away a near neighbour uncertain. Most land around the lake had been parcelled out in cottage lots of years ago. Cottagers are seasonal. Some come for Christmas or a weekend in winter. Most board up their cottages on the last day of August and reappear in June. It was a deep long winter Harry had by himself with his dog and his two horses and his subscription to the *National Geographic*. Snow drifted up to the eaves. His hay wagon got him to town every two weeks for supplies. He ate tins of corned beef hash and green peas and coffee. He liked now and then an O'Henry chocolate bar. Until probably the middle of May he lived in two rooms of the farmhouse namely the kitchen (which had the stove) and the bedroom directly above it (which had the stovepipe). Other rooms whispered with ice.

And then three months in summer Harry's world filled suddenly up. The cottagers came back and so did we. Who's we. Harry was the brother of my father's mother Ethel. Ethel had four children including my father and they all had children and the children all had friends. Week after week in summer these people arrived in groups of three to ten. The idea was to 'help Harry bring in the hay' this was the phrase they used and enjoy a vacation at the lake. The idea was not Harry's. I never heard him comment on it. He did comment on the inability of my father and my uncles to master scything technique. Harry could scythe 100 square metres of hay in three and a half minutes leaving a patch as level as his moustache with fallen stalks unbruised. There was frustration and a redfaced man in the hayfield many an afternoon. Harry remained unfailingly polite to everyone. So did the dog (whose name was Shep although it was a succession of dogs) so did the horses (Prince and Florence who were immortal at that time).

CHORUS 1:

The horses were apparently immortal

CHORUS 2:

The horses were usually immortal

CHORUS 3:

The horses were to some extent immortal

CHORUS 4:

And the fur smelled of violence

T

CHORUS 1, 2:
Very old winter violence

CHORUS 3, 4:
Now worn by young girls

CHORUS 1, 2, 3, 4:
Explain why this matters

CHORUS 1, 2:
Trembling oh the bells

CHORUS 1:
Oh the bells that were stirring were not the same

CHORUS 2:
Why the bells were the bells were

CHORUS 1, 2, 3, 4:
Not the same

CHORUS 1:
Explain bells

CHORUS 2:
Explain girls

CHORUS 1, 2, 3, 4:
Explain very old trembling

CHORUS 1:
Were girls the same

CHORUS 1, 2, 3, 4:
Oh very

CHORUS 1:
Were horses

T

CHORUS 1, 2, 3, 4:
Oh very

CHORUS 1:
Were bells oh the bells oh the bells that were trembling were not the same

[all snap masks]

LECTURER:
THE GEOGRAPHIC
When Harry died in a psychiatric hospital at the age of 94 my father went to clear
out the farmhouse. All the rooms except the kitchen were packed floor to ceiling
with issues of the NATIONAL GEOGRAPHIC.

CHORUS 1, 2, 3, 4:
How many natural phenomena are there

LECTURER:
From the door to the bed in Harry's bedroom a narrow channel had been left open
and another around the stovepipe. The smell you can imagine.

CHORUS 1, 2:
Volcano and say so
As often and say so

LECTURER:
Now if you had ever met Harry the one thing you would say is that he was someone
who knew a lot of things about a lot of things. He knew about haying and horses and
weather but also the history of violins or where to build a canal or volcanoes in Papua
New Guinea. How he got this way was a mystery as he left school at age 15 the year
he went deaf.

CHORUS 3, 4:
He is easily curious
He exactly remembers

LECTURER:
He had few books in his house and no public library anywhere around there. Certainly
he read the NATIONAL GEOGRAPHIC from cover to cover.

CHORUS 1, 2, 3, 4:

There is no use whatsoever all winter long

LECTURER:

His mind gave excitement to everything he read and it entered into his will to live.

CHORUS 1, 2, 3:

No noise no potato

CHORUS 4:

However a volcano

LECTURER:

Living for Harry was knowing how things work. This was the happiest he could be.

CHORUS 1, 2:

Repeat potato

CHORUS 3, 4:

Repeat volcano

CHORUS 4:

Repeat the happiest he could be

CHORUS 1, 2, 3, 4:

The happiest he could be

[all snap masks]

LECTURER:

ETHEL

Ethel was big. Ethel was six feet tall. Bony. Rigorous. Her husband had a heart attack in a department store on a Toronto day in 1932. There were four young children. Ethel went to work cleaning other people's houses. I remember her huge hands and the smell of Noxzema on her skin. Every day a clean housedress a clean apron. There is one photograph of her standing by the lake with Harry just after the war in trousers and sunlight. She has a barrette in her hair and an expression bounding forth like joy but it is untypical.

T

CHORUS 1, 2, 3, 4:

How many natural phenomena are there

CHORUS 1, 2:

Volcano and say so

No noise no potato

CHORUS 3, 4:

He is easily curious

He exactly remembers

CHORUS 1, 2, 3, 4:

There is no use whatsoever all winter long

CHORUS 1, 2:

Repeat potato

CHORUS 3, 4:

Repeat volcano

CHORUS 2:

Repeat the happiest he could be

CHORUS 1, 2, 3, 4:

The happiest he could be

[all snap masks]

LECTURER:

As Harry's elder sister Ethel felt responsible for seeing him through the summer when his world got complicated. She stayed from June to September. There was a reordering of Harry's life. Three meals a day. Clean underwear. No cursing. There were points on which they agreed to disagree like Harry's admiration for starting the day with a tot of whiskey. He had his little low shelf behind the chair where he always sat at the head of the kitchen table. A dusty bit of old green leather tacked over it for privacy. Harry rose at five in the morning to light the stove. Ethel slept till five–thirty. He usually got his whiskey. But she absolutely forbade him to eat peas off his knife. Another skill he had perfected. I remember sitting with cousins uncles aunts around the kitchen table on a sweltering summer noon. Bowls steamed on the red

plaid oilcloth. Meat mashed potatoes carrots green peas. A good hot lunch Ethel said.
Up at his end of the table Harry sat peacefully lining up peas on his knife. He filled
the length of the blade with single–file peas and raised it to his open mouth and shot
it with a motion like a sword swallower. Never a pea was spilled. *Harry!* flew from
Ethel's end of the table. Then Harry tipped the peas off his knife and sat quietly. Or
reached up with one hand removed the hearing aid from his ear laid it by his plate.
Went back to lining up peas on his knife.

CHORUS I:

When they go he will be different

CHORUS 2:

And it was promised that all the arrangement

CHORUS 3:

Might move from right to left

CHORUS 4:

That all the arrangement afterward

CHORUS I, 2, 3, 4:

Promise it they say

CHORUS 4:

Remembering the cold

CHORUS I:

When they go he will be different

CHORUS 2:

Afterward they say

CHORUS 4:

Was he right

CHORUS 3:

Was he left

T

CHORUS 2, 3, 4:
Was he after all

CHORUS 1:
Out in the cold

[all snap masks]

LECTURER:
THE ODD QUESTION

Was he vain about being a hermit asked my friend Ben and I thought *What an odd question* – it made me laugh. Uncle Harry being the least vain person I ever met and hermit not a word he would use. He liked being alone. He had one good suit a black suit that he wore annually to visit the Canadian National Exhibition in Toronto at the end of August. He went alone by train. He viewed all the exhibits tried all the samples and came back the same night. He was buried in the black suit.

CHORUS 1:
Vanity is no defence

CHORUS 2:
A lake is a defence

CHORUS 3:
A laugh is a defence

CHORUS 4:
They did not defend him nor did I

[all snap masks]

LECTURER:
THE LAUGH

He had a rough square laugh like characters in comics who say HAAR HAAR HAAR. Laughs came out his face sideways over his pipe somehow this adding to the hilariousness as if his whole being had slipped out on a jag – 'sudden glory' as Hobbes says of laughter.

CHORUS 1:
Vanity is no defence

CHORUS 2:

A lake is a defence

CHORUS 3:

A laugh is a defence

CHORUS 4:

They did not defend him nor did I

CHORUS 1:

Meanwhile snow came at an angle

CHORUS 2:

It was more than a pleasure to go

CHORUS 3:

To go on with my life a state apart

CHORUS 1, 2, 3:

And to whom would there be an obligation

CHORUS 4:

To whom would the commas feel like cattle brands

[all snap masks]

LECTURER:

THE LAKE

The lake was a masterpiece. I loved it like a person. It had birch trees slipping themselves silver in the wind along the shore silver in itself and situations of water lilies both sides of the dock tangling to a swimmer. I swam all day. We all swam whenever we weren't having to do anything else. Harry didn't swim. He had lost his hearing by diving fast and deep into the lake when he was 15 rupturing an eardrum. On very hot afternoons he would come down from the barn and sit on the shore to take the breeze a while.

There is something else to tell about this lake that I thought of as Uncle Harry's lake although on maps it had the name Paint. Once I had surgery. Afterwards things went awry what doctors call complications. I lay for some days and nights in a hospital cloud of pain. Then there was a fifth night and something rose up. I can't call

T

it a dream it didn't seem to me I was asleep. I can call it a visitation from the devil. The devil took this form. A sequence of TV screens came forward one after another behind my closed eyes. As one came another disappeared as another came. Each screen had some bright fast story gibbering and grabbing itself along so TV does and we are accustomed to this but each story had also a quality I can only describe as evil I mean an entire human coldness a cruelty like an essence of torture. I call it a devil. Each TV glowed out at me a consciousness that wanted to suck me into its evil.

It Was Black, Black Took says Gertrude Stein somewhere and black in the sense of a life-or-death contest going on. The only action I could put against the pull of this was to insert myself into Uncle Harry's lake and swim continually backwards and out backwards and out away from each screen as it approached away from that suck of death worst where I swam hour after hour placing myself into the red stalks of the water lilies shifting their weight in the vast silence of underwater here to there here to there placing myself pushing myself back away from the devil and the stench of death pouring out of TV screens filling every molecule of the night except for swimming. At some point it ended or I awoke it was like being washed out of hell. This account sounds melodramatic to you I imagine. However I am also sure that in the grit and dregs at the bottom of the psyche where pain has its kitchen there are only extremes there is no mildness there is no mercy. Mercy is from a lake or from an uncle. Having no sense of time at the time I later calculated the night in the lake to be a Wednesday. Wednesday made me think again about Uncle Harry and loneliness. It was not pleasant to think about before. It was not pleasant to be specific. Now the parts change. I see him a Wednesday night in his kitchen looking out the back window on black January black silence black snow. I see him turn and go to the stove and take off the stove lid and stir the embers with an old poker that hangs on a hook on the side of the stove and his face gets hot. He stares down into the fire. He is at the centre of a reasonable kingdom. He does not often think about another. Another what. Exactly.

CHORUS 1:

If the week had one Wednesday

CHORUS 2:

If the month had four Wednesdays

CHORUS 3:

If the year had fifty-two Wednesdays

CHORUS 4:

If TV had 10,000 Wednesdays

T

CHORUS 1, 2, 3, 4:
And they all came on the same night

CHORUS 4:
You might prefer to be shot dead

CHORUS 3:
What good's your uncle to you now they said

CHORUS 2:
You need something to smoke and something to chew better already

CHORUS 1:
I'd suggest taking off that red scarf with a very little example

CHORUS 3:
It's a very little example

CHORUS 1, 2, 3, 4:
Exactly they said

[all snap masks]

LECTURER:

THE ICE

The most impressive tools that Uncle Harry owned – surpassing even his scythe
which in the hands of someone who knows how to use it is an instrument of almost
supernatural grace and clarity as you may know if you've ever seen anyone scything
– were his ice tongs. A pair of tongs as big as himself that hung sideways on a hook
outside the ice house. Harry needed a small income. Part of it came from selling lots
to cottagers. Part of it came from building them cottages. After that he started his
ice business. Ice is a staple of summer life. Nobody bothers with a refrigerator at the
lake – you could never get one delivered that far up north anyway fridges take too
much electricity. Most people had an icebox in the cellar. An icebox needs a block of
ice every so often. In late April Harry went out on the lake with Prince and Florence
and cut one-metre square blocks out of it. Using his tongs he hoisted them onto the
hay wagon. Prince and Florence hauled it up the path to the ice house. Harry tonged
the blocks off the wagon into the ice house wrapped in dry gold sawdust and straw
and didn't they look grand. All summer he delivered blocks of ice up and down the

T

road. Odd he had no icebox of his own. Every day just before noon I was sent out to the creek behind the house to pull up a bottle of milk from between two rocks where water got deep and rushed along. I must have tried to bite the glass one day because it is a memory I have in my teeth and lips and hands the glass-hard chill of it.

Another thing about ice. This came after his death. During his life I was never at the farm in April so I did not hear what must have been an annual event for Harry although as a deaf man he would have processed it differently than I do – have you ever gone to a Stevie Wonder concert and watched deaf children in the front row lay their heads and arms on the stage to get the sound – by means of what is called infrasonic vibrations. When the ice goes out there is a gigantic pluck as if a bowstring stretched deep under the ice from end to end of the lake had some vast finger pluck it once. A vibration shoots across from shore to shore. If you are standing anywhere near you vibrate too. It feels low and long and strange like an animal stare.

CHORUS 1:
Do you like the word infrasonic

CHORUS 2:
Let's evolve it

CHORUS 3:
Become Gertrude Stein on sabbatical

CHORUS 1, 2, 4:
Now you are infragrammatical

CHORUS 3:
If you're Harry's scythe shaped like a harp

CHORUS 2:
You'll be infrasharp

CHORUS 3:
If you're one of Harry's nephews from the city

CHORUS 2, 4:
You'll infrahuff and infrapuff your way through the hayfield arousing pity

T

CHORUS 1:

Become Harry's knife

CHORUS 2:

Infra green peas and strife

CHORUS 3:

Become James Joyce (go on be brazen)

CHORUS 4:

You'll find yourself inventing the word infrahuman

CHORUS 1, 2:

Become Prince and Florence

CHORUS 3, 4:

But there I can't go

CHORUS 1:

It's nice to imagine that we can imagine our way into anything living and real

CHORUS 1, 2, 3, 4:

But no

CHORUS 1:

It just isn't so

[all snap masks]

LECTURER:

THE REPAIR

Uncle Harry was good at repair rethinking rearrangement. His eyeglasses held together with tape at the corners and wads of paper under the pads that press either side of the nose leaving a red mark. His socks overalls truck the pump beside the kitchen sink had each been refashioned were each by now a collection. I can't see when I move through the rooms of the farmhouse in memory anything there that was new and shiny. The objects he used had no indolence in them none of that lazy disregarding storebought glow. They were heavy with work and always clean. Later an era of neglect set in. Harry got old. Nobody spent their vacation at the farm anymore

T

because of dirt and his moods came on sudden. Prince and Florence died. The barn was unsafe. My father went up north in winter and came back angry and sad. *He has to leave that farm* he would say. *Nobody can tell Harry anything* he would say. Finally Harry got gangrene in his leg. There was a family consultation of everybody not Harry. Everybody not Harry decided. My father and his two brothers went up north and took Harry out of the farmhouse into hospital. The gangrene healed but Harry's dementia impressed the doctors. He was transferred to a psychiatric ward and never went home again.

I remember visiting him at the hospital with my father. The psychiatric ward was separated from the rest of the building by solid walls of steel mesh and a difference of lighting. Uncle Harry stood in a total fury. I don't recall anything else. I don't believe he spoke. We left him in his bright room. My father vanished into the warden's office while I waited on a chair. Years later after both Harry and my father were dead I found in my father's desk a folder of letters from this warden. Each contained an itemised bill for sheets and blankets. Whenever sheets and blankets had been given to Harry he tore them apart with his hands.

Natural phenomena make it difficult not to look says Gertrude Stein but can we not look. Can we change the sentence.

CHORUS 3:
A sentence says you know what I mean

[all snap masks]

LECTURER:
Can we go back to a moment when he was living and clean and there still were things in the world he thought he could repair. The following happened one autumn. Harry was at the beginning of getting old. One of my father's brothers whose name was Ken decided Harry would be better off to leave the farm and come live in suburbia. Ken had a ranch-style house with a guestroom 400 or so miles away from Harry's farm. How Ken persuaded Harry into the car no one knew.

CHORUS 3:
A sentence says

CHORUS 4:
A sentence says

T

CHORUS 3, 4:

A sentence says you know what I mean

CHORUS 2:

Suppose a lone man

LECTURER:

Maybe he said it was just a visit. They drove south. Soon Harry was standing in the guest room looking out on Ken's back patio with its barbecue and clipped cedar hedge. He didn't sleep. Some days and nights went by.

CHORUS 1, 3, 4:

A sentence says you know what I mean

CHORUS 2:

How are you at grinding

CHORUS 3:

How are you at hours

CHORUS 1, 2, 4:

How are you at that door

LECTURER:

At midnight he dressed in his black suit a clean white shirt a tie. He let himself out the patio door and stood on the lawn a while. He took in the night its sway its way of cocking. He got his bearings. He set off north crossing backyards peony beds other people's sleep. He walked in the direction of the lake.

[person folding sheets upstage goes downstage centre with sheet and begins ripping sheet slowly in pieces, continuing to end]

CHORUS 1:

Did we neglect persecution

CHORUS 2:

Glass makes ground glass

CHORUS I:

Suppose a family

CHORUS 4:

Keep away from that door dear

CHORUS 2:

There follows a question which is not a question

CHORUS I:

A family has useful knowledge

CHORUS 4:

Keep away from that door dear

CHORUS 2:

How are you at hours

CHORUS 3:

A sentence says you know what I mean

CHORUS I, 2, 3, 4:

Suppose you don't

CHORUS 2:

Suppose a family

CHORUS I, 2, 3:

Suppose a lone man broke forests and had an extra sun

CHORUS 4:

Keep away from that door dear

CHORUS I, 2, 3:

Keep away from that door dear

CHORUS I, 2, 3, 4:

How are you at keeping away from that door

T

CHORUS 3:

And to whom would the commas feel like cattle brands

[all snap masks]

LECTURER:

Do we need a finale
Everyone needs a finale
The finale

CHORUS 2, 3, 4

He was a full one living

CHORUS 2:

He seized it when he saw it

CHORUS 3

A most beautiful sound

CHORUS 2, 3, 4:

Is the sound of what happens

CHORUS 1:

Can you repeat that

CHORUS 2, 3, 4:

I am going to do so

CHORUS 3:

Explain why this matters

CHORUS 3:

I am going to do so

CHORUS 4:

There is an intensity of movement

CHORUS 2, 3, 4:

Combined with not seeming to be getting anywhere

T

CHORUS 1:

Can you repeat that

CHORUS 2, 3, 4:

No. This is the end.

CHORUS 1:

There is not such an end.

[person ripping sheet drops pieces and bows to audience from the waist, deeply, once and during brief blackout exits]

INTERVIEW

WITH

ROSALIND E. KRAUSS

HAVING A DRINK with a legendary art critic in a café next door to the Centre Pompidou is an anxiety-inducing prospect. Should I visit the museum beforehand, I wondered, just in case one of the shows comes up, so as to be prepared? But then, maybe she'll say something inspiring that will change the way I'd look at a given show, so maybe I should wait? Should I know what's at the Venice Biennale? Should I reread *S/Z*? Should I be *au courant* with every piece ever published in *OCTOBER*, the avant-garde journal she co-founded in 1976?

These are just a few of the things I worried about before meeting Rosalind E. Krauss, the mention of whose name can make the most polished art historian stutter in awe, thinking of the way she stood up to her mentor Clement Greenberg, her perspicacity, her theoretical breadth, those iconic photos of her from the sixties, especially the one, in profile, with her chin resting on her typewriter, when she was barely thirty years old, taken by Ann Gabhart. ('Spare me smart Jewish girls with their typewriters,' Greenberg said to Krauss in 1974.) It felt like as soon as I arrived at Columbia University as an undergraduate I was hearing her name; since then, as a scholar researching in the field of modernism and visual culture, her work on surrealism and photography has had an enormous influence on my critical approach.

I settled for looking back over her essay collections and attentively reading her most recent book, *UNDER BLUE CUP* (2011), a text that blends art criticism, theory and autobiographical writing inspired by the cognitive therapy she underwent as a result of an aneurysm in 1999. Taking up the chessboard as the quintessential 'support' for art, the book proposes a series of 'white knights', heroes of Krauss's who are defending the making of art as a bounded, rigorous practice: Ed Ruscha, Jamie Coleman, Richard Serra, Sophie Calle, William Kentridge, among others. It features a wicked brand of humour and a lighter touch less in evidence in her more scholarly writing. For those who are unfamiliar with her work, *UNDER BLUE CUP* provides a way in; as Krauss moves through so much of her work in an exercise in remembering, she also works through her central tenets as an art critic. 'The medium makes you who you are,' she told the *OBSERVER* when the book was published. 'And thinking about this sense of who you are brought me back to my personal experience.'

Which in turn brought me back to my own experience, and my own medium: language. I am not an art historian, so elected to engage with her not as a specialist in her work but as a critic in my own right, capable of contextualising her work within the culture at large. I came to see that one of her most important contributions has been to rethink the dynamics by which we think about medium, the ways in which we emphasise and define the tension between form and play. *UNDER BLUE CUP*'s point of departure is the coupling of disparate images, the way this does something to the brain, reminding us that in everyday life we naturalise this oddity. In its attack on routinised forms of art, Krauss's work suggests a way for us to see things anew.

———————

^{Q.} THE WHITE REVIEW — You have a new book out in 2016, *WILLEM DE KOONING NONSTOP: CHERCHEZ LA FEMME*.

^{A.} ROSALIND E. KRAUSS — I decided to write that when I was going through MoMA's de Kooning show [in 2011–12]. I went with a friend of mine who wanted me to be her guide. So I was explaining the 'Woman' paintings to her, and then as I was listening to myself I thought *this is really interesting*. The book is about the formal intelligence of the work, the way it repeats over and over and over again. I suppose you could call it a formalist book, except I hate the word 'formalist'.

^{Q.} THE WHITE REVIEW — Why is that?

^{A.} ROSALIND E. KRAUSS — Formalism has got a bad rap, but you can't really talk about art unless you talk about the formal intelligence behind the work. That's how work signifies, so formalist is an important word.

^{Q.} THE WHITE REVIEW — You conclude the introductory essay to your collection *BACHELORS* (1999) by writing: 'art made by women needs no special pleading, and in the essays that follow I will offer none'. Why, then, write a book about art made by women?

^{A.} ROSALIND E. KRAUSS — I didn't write a book, I just realised that I had all these essays on women. I thought feminism was kind of a pain, it was a bit coercive, and so I decided as a sort of joke, an ironic gesture, to collect my essays on women. One of them was on a work by Sherrie Levine, called *BACHELORS: 1–6* (1991), and that's included in the book, so that's where I got the name. There were seven or eight essays in the book and then my editor at MIT Press, Roger Conover, said if you're going to call it *BACHELORS* you've got to have nine [a reference to the 1939 Sacha Guitry film *NINE BACHELORS*]. So that's why I included Claude

Cahun as the introduction, to make nine bachelors. I just decided that it was kind of fun to do it.

^{Q.} THE WHITE REVIEW — *OCTOBER* is such a bold publishing project. How did it start?

^{A.} ROSALIND E. KRAUSS — I worked for a long time and was on the board of editors at *ARTFORUM*. Phil Leider, who was this brilliant editor, left *ARTFORUM* and installed in his place this absolute creep named John Coplans, who set about destroying the magazine. At a certain point, Annette Michelson, one of the other members of the editorial board, and I decided we had to leave, and that we would start a new magazine. And it was called *OCTOBER*, after the Eisenstein film. From the time it started until ten years into it, *OCTOBER* was funded by the National Endowment for the Arts, and then suddenly they stopped funding. There were terrible cutbacks and then they stopped funding publications. So our money ran out, and I was having a coffee with Sherrie Levine, and I said *OCTOBER*'s finished, and she said 'no no no don't say that', and she said 'the way you'll stay afloat is to publish portfolios of photographs, we'll give you the photographs,' and she meant herself and other artists – Cindy Sherman, Louise Lawlor, Laurie Simmons. So in a sense *OCTOBER*'s been funded by women.

^{Q.} THE WHITE REVIEW — How did you decide on an editorial line?

^{A.} ROSALIND E. KRAUSS — We decided it pretty much on the basis of what John Coplans refused to publish: anything having to do with European art, or theory – he was very involved in making money for the magazine, so therefore in sponsoring whatever galleries were supporting it. He wouldn't hear of publishing anything on performance, or video,

or film, because none of the galleries would support that. We also decided not to have any colour, because that was one of the very expensive things that ARTFORUM did, nor would we have advertising. So we just made it the flip side of everything bad about ARTFORUM.

Q. THE WHITE REVIEW —— So it was initially funded, or part-funded, by the NEA, and eventually you diversified your publications to make more money.

A. ROSALIND E. KRAUSS —— First we had the NEA, and then at a certain point there was a foundation by Armand and Celeste Bartos, wealthy patrons of the arts, and then they funded us for a while, and then that stopped. Then we started our portfolios, and something called October Files, these little monographic books of what we consider to be the best critical writing on a given artist. The first was on Richard Serra, and then James Coleman, and Lichtenstein, and Warhol, and these have been extremely successful. Our idea was that we would publish these for extremely low prices so that students could afford to buy them. We made a deal with MIT Press, which publishes them: a buck a book. I was tired of dealing with royalty statements from university presses – it's creative accounting, you can never tell how the amount of money you get paid has anything to do with how many books you sell. So I said: you sell a book, you give us a dollar. And it worked. They sold 2,100 books, we got $2,100.

Q. THE WHITE REVIEW —— How did it wind up being published by MIT Press?

A. ROSALIND E. KRAUSS —— At the beginning we had a strong relationship with Peter Eisenman, who was director of the Institute for Architecture and Urban studies, and they had a magazine called OPPOSITIONS. They had a deal with MIT Press, so in a sense through them we had this relationship. For a while we were closely affiliated with Eisenman and his team and also with the architects who were teaching at Princeton – Michael Graves, Richard Meier, and Eisenman.

Q. THE WHITE REVIEW —— In recent years the concept of modernism has been re-theorised and re-conceived in literary studies; has this reached your field as well?

A. ROSALIND E. KRAUSS —— UNDER BLUE CUP really is my way of restating the central tenet of modernism, which I take to be medium specificity. It's an attempt to retrieve the concept and centrality of the medium in the face of its abandonment by post-modernism. To do that I had to think of ways of describing or instituting medium that weren't just about the traditional forms – oil painting, or marble or bronze sculpture, all of these mediums that have fallen out of use, out of favour. So I thought, how can I talk about the medium, which is the support of the representation, without just falling back on the traditional medium? That's how I got into this idea of 'technical support'. It seemed to me that artists are dealing with new supports. Ruscha's medium, for example, being a car.

Q. THE WHITE REVIEW —— UNDER BLUE CUP is both about recuperating your memory after your aneurysm and recuperating a version of modernism that has been forgotten.

A. ROSALIND E. KRAUSS —— I thought of it as a conceit that would open up, and that's where the title comes from – this flash card I was shown during my cognitive therapy. What they tell you is that if you can remember who you are, you can teach yourself to remember anything.

Art | Theory | Criticism | Politics

OCTOBER

37

$6.00/Summer 1986   Published by the MIT Press

Q. THE WHITE REVIEW — You write about how, after your aneurysm, your therapist showed you disparate images to try to coax forth thought, like 'a tennis pro paired with a zipper, or a football player teamed with a yo-yo'. You work in what you call a structuralist mode, citing one thing and then its opposite. It reminds me of the surrealist concept of the marvelous as the meeting on the dissecting table of an umbrella and a sewing machine.

A. ROSALIND E. KRAUSS — I am a tennis player, and I can tell you, you don't wear clothes with zippers, because the sweat corrodes the metal. I found UNDER BLUE CUP fun to write. I wrote it in a personal way because I wanted it to be reader-friendly. I thought that many of my books were too dense or peculiar for people to follow, but this autobiographical form is something that people can get into.

Q. THE WHITE REVIEW — How do you approach the idea of genre in your writing, as an art critic?

A. ROSALIND E. KRAUSS — As an art critic I have to say that the breakthrough I had was when Arne Glimcher, the director of Pace Gallery, came up to me at one point and said he was having this show on grids, and would I write something for the catalogue? I said yes and then thought – what is there to say about grids? What a boring topic! But, well, maybe I can make something out of the repetition of grids, and the boringness of it. And that's when I thought of this wonderful Lévi-Strauss essay on the structural anthropology of myth, and it seemed to me that what he says about myth, that it repeats over and over again because there's some kind of contradiction that cannot be solved, that can only be repeated. I thought, that sounds like what I know about grids, so that's when my art criticism began to be related to and supported by what I had read,

and structuralism and post-structuralism. My reading of Georges Bataille led me to the idea of the formless.

Q. THE WHITE REVIEW — I love this notion of the *informe*, what you call in BACHELORS a 'categorical blurring [...] initiated by the continual alteration of identity'. This structuralist tension between oppositions.

A. ROSALIND E. KRAUSS — Bill Rubin asked me to contribute to a catalogue when he did a huge show called 'PRIMITIVISM' IN 20TH CENTURY ART [MoMA, 1984]. He asked me to write about Giacometti, and writing about Giacometti and primitivism was very difficult. Finally I started reading Denis Hollier's book on Georges Bataille, and I understood that Bataille's magazine DOCUMENTS had a dictionary, and one of the definitions was for the word *informe* [formless]. I began to see the relationship between what happens in Giacometti's work and this idea of the formless. And so it took off in relationship to that. The formless is very important to a book I wrote called THE OPTICAL UNCONSCIOUS (1993), written out of a reaction to Clement Greenberg, and the dogmas that had overtaken art criticism and art writing related to him.

Q. THE WHITE REVIEW — What were you trying to overthrow, or undermine?

A. ROSALIND E. KRAUSS — It was this teleological reading of history in which everything would end up in this idea of the optical, the dissolve of matter into pure, almost hallucinatory visual non-substance, almost a mirage. That's the way Greenberg talked about Jackson Pollock, and also Michael Fried, and so the idea of the optical unconscious was really to combat this notion of the mirage. I wanted to bring forward a kind of libidinal unconscious that made this optical mirage impossible, which I saw as a sort of sublimated form of art. It would de-sublimate it, that's what the optical unconscious was about. I took the name in a way from Fred Jameson's book THE POLITICAL UNCONSCIOUS (1981), but also from Walter Benjamin, who at a certain point talks about the optical unconscious in relation to photography.

Q. THE WHITE REVIEW —— I'm stuck on Clement Greenberg's teleological progression: is it the sort of thing you learn in Modern Art 101, the movement of form - planes, lines, the grid - becoming slowly more abstract through Mondrian to Rothko and then Pollock?

A. ROSALIND E. KRAUSS —— In a way, except abstraction puts a different twist on it. The movement toward abstraction is a move towards the reflexive presentation of the material substrate of the work: the frame, the canvas. Abstraction is not really optical in that sense, but material. Greenberg moves through abstraction into this idea of the non-material, the optical. He talks about David Smith's sculpture being unsupported; he likens the matter of sculpture to modernist architecture, and to the grids of modernist architecture that don't seem to be supported by anything. Reading it, you see this drive towards the optical and the non-material.

Q. THE WHITE REVIEW —— So you're trying to bring back in the material support that underpins the work.

A. ROSALIND E. KRAUSS —— Yes, because the idea of the libidinal brings in the body, and the pulses and feelings that belong to it.

Q. THE WHITE REVIEW —— Speaking of material supports, I picked up on a lot of references to chessboards across your work, on Giacometti,

or in UNDER BLUE CUP for instance, where you write about the knight's move. I think that's such a wonderful image because it brings up both the material support but also the constraint of the game.

A. ROSALIND E. KRAUSS —— For me, chess became the natural analogy to the idea of the support. I had a breakthrough - with the idea of these heroes of mine who would move across the chessboard - at a William Kentridge show at MACBA [Museu d'Art Contemporani de Barcelona, 1999]. I had this revelation in front of his wonderful film 'Ubu Tells the Truth' (1997), in which these prisoners are falling down from the roof of Johannesburg prison past these windows that seem to be rising behind them. I thought, that's like the film's frames spooling back into the projector, and it seemed to me that it was an absolute presentation of the image of film.

Q. THE WHITE REVIEW —— You also write about this idea of medium awareness in an essay on Vito Acconci, when he points at the centre of the screen: video pointing to itself. That seems like an important aspect of your concept of the technical support of a work. At the same time you have written against a sense of art that expands out in all directions, and the importance of recognising sculpture as a 'historically bounded field' and not something that bleeds into all materials all the time. In that sense, one of your bêtes noires is installation art.

A. ROSALIND E. KRAUSS —— Well, it just seems to me to be a falsely seductive appeal to viewers, without any formal rigour at all. I guess I can't say anything more than that. I just hate seeing these little video monitors set up that you're supposed to look into.

Q. THE WHITE REVIEW —— To come back to the idea of medium more specifically, at one point in your book on Marcel Broodthaers, *A VOYAGE ON THE NORTH SEA* (1999), you talk about wanting to throw out the term 'medium' 'like so much critical toxic waste'. More recently, in works like *UNDER BLUE CUP* and *PERPETUAL INVENTORY* (2010), you write against what you call a 'post-medium' condition. Why is this category so important?

A. ROSALIND E. KRAUSS — I like the word 'medium'. I said that in order to underscore the way that medium had become polluted for critical discourse, and that in order to bring it back you had to do a lot of work. For me, medium is a very important term, it short-circuits a lot of other verbiage. Somebody who talks about the problem of using the term medium is Stanley Cavell, and what he uses instead is the term 'automatism'. What he's really talking about is like in music, the way that certain music feels improvised, there's a sort of form, a substratum, that exists under the music, that moves from key to key. If you think about Mozart, it sounds improvised, because of the way he's moving through these various transitions. That's what Cavell is talking about: at a certain point music becomes automatic, because it has this form of transition that means that you can improvise over it.

Q. THE WHITE REVIEW — Because you're always governed by an underlying grid that's controlling what you can do within that frame.

A. ROSALIND E. KRAUSS — I like that idea of trying to find another term for medium the way he uses automatism, and that was when I got to the thought of structural support, which seemed to fit what I was talking about in terms of Ruscha and Christian Marclay. Marclay's 'Video Quartet' (2002) is really wonderful. There are these four DVDs that are spaced out along the wall and each TV is playing the film, and those films look as though they're moving vertically, but the panorama of them is horizontal. They're mostly musical things, all sound films, people playing the piano, or the sound of music. For me the great moment was when at a certain point a bunch of cockroaches runs over the keys and you're suddenly transported back to silent film. That's the way the idea of the technical support of film is made visual, made available.

Q. THE WHITE REVIEW — What's your sense of the most interesting questions artists are asking, or should be asking, at the moment? If you could commission a piece what would it be?

A. ROSALIND E. KRAUSS — I don't think I could do that. Whatever Kentridge or Richard Serra comes up with, I think oh, that's worth doing.

Q. THE WHITE REVIEW — I wanted to ask you a bit about critical method. In *THE ORIGINALITY OF THE AVANT-GARDE AND OTHER MODERNIST MYTHS* (1986), you consider the question of whether 'the interest of critical writing lies almost entirely in its method'. You then go on to contend that any discussion of value is 'in fact the product of what a given method allows one to ask or even to think of asking.' I want to ask about the way your attitude towards method has changed since that early book – what kind of methodology do you strive for?

A. ROSALIND E. KRAUSS — That book started with the grids essay, and includes 'Sculpture in the Expanded Field'. Both took up their subjects in relation to structuralism, and the structuralist method allows for a total breakthrough in what can be talked about, and how it can be developed clearly. For me, clarity is the most important thing in writing about art. And so 'Sculpture in the Expanded Field', like 'Grids', began with the thought, 'What is there to say about this? It's impossible.' The essay

had to do with the fact that sculpture seemed
to be all over the place, and people would talk
about it in terms of the idea of plurality, which
is a term I absolutely hate, because it assumes
you can do anything. I'm like [art historian
Heinrich] Wölfflin, I do not think everything
can be done at any one time. History controls
what can be done at any given time, so I hated
this idea of sculptural plurality, earthworks,
institutional critique, blah blah blah. So I de-
cided to find a way to control the way the field
operated, so the connections between these
works were logical. That was a structuralist
term again.

Q. THE WHITE REVIEW — If your goal is a
clarity that structuralist thought brings, what
are your feelings toward post-structuralism?
Does it just muddy the waters?

A. ROSALIND E. KRAUSS — Not at all. I've
learned a tremendous amount from Derrida
and various post-structuralist figures. I teach
a course at Columbia called 'Modernism,
Structuralism, Post-Structuralism', and the
students find that very difficult to say, so they
call it PMS. Isn't that wonderful? So the first
lecture I always say, I know you call this PMS,
and I find that as funny as you do.

LAUREN ELKIN, JULY 2015

MONOLOGUE FROM THE 11th FLOOR

BY

ALICJA KWADE

XXIX, XXX

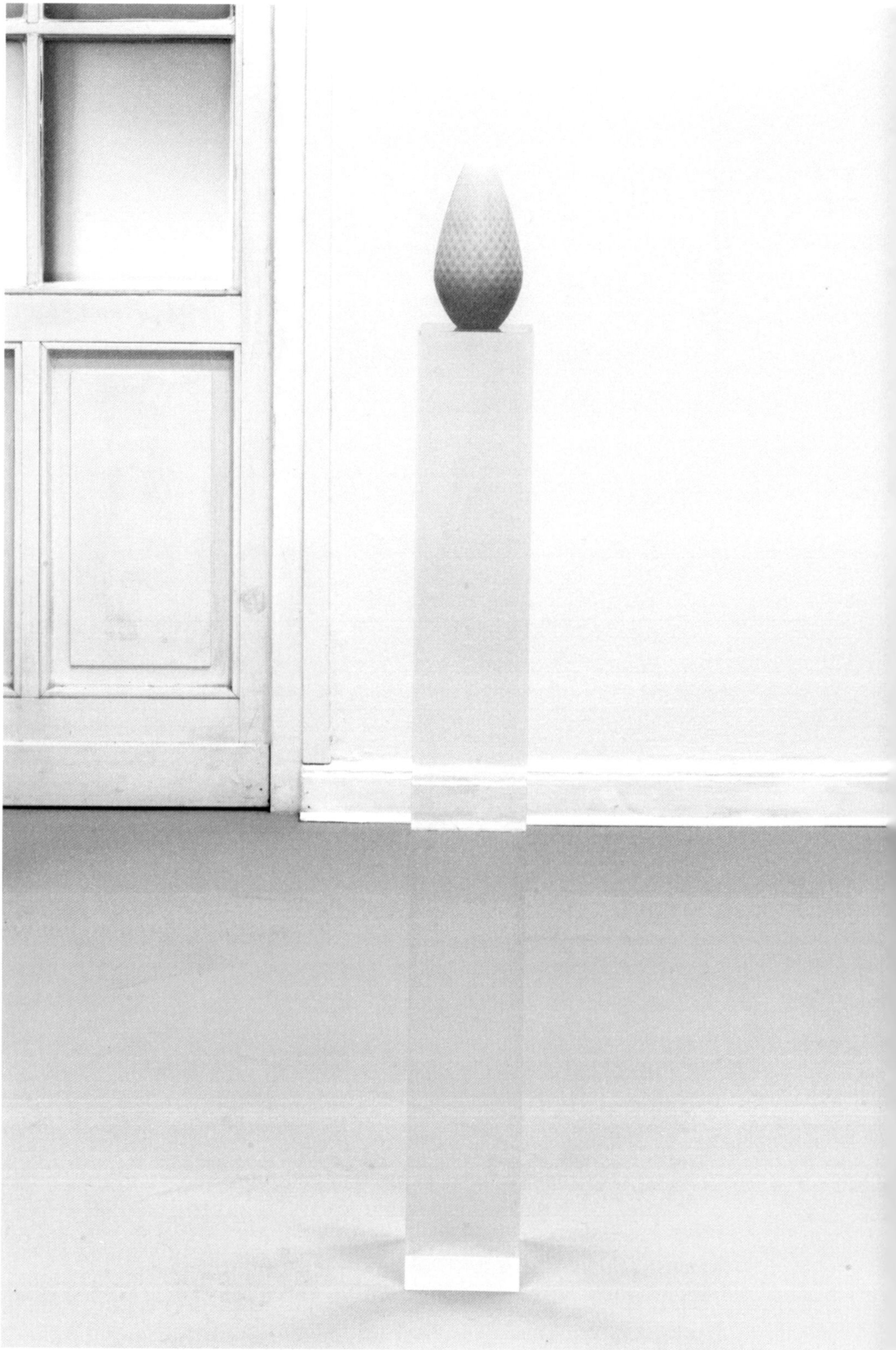

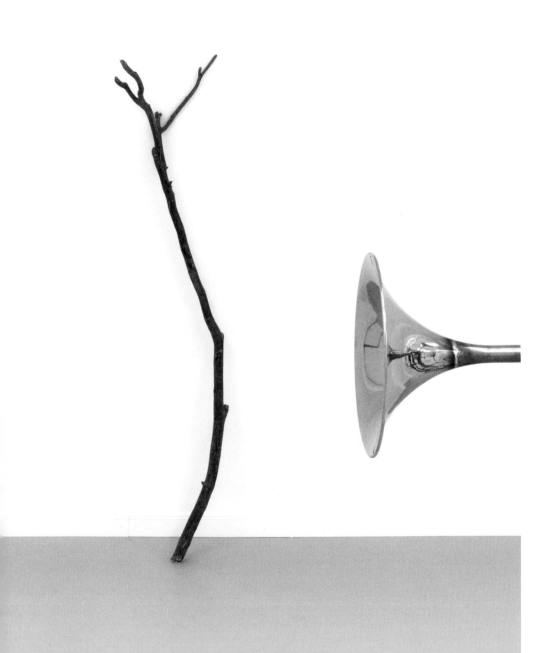

TWO PILGRIMS

BY

LÁSZLÓ KRASZNAHORKAI

(*tr.* OTTILIE MULZET)

THEY HAVE BEEN TRAVELLING for more than four hours when suddenly the asphalt comes to an end. The bus proceeds along a bumpy dirt road, then one half-hour later crosses below a Communist-era triumphal arch made out of concrete: for a moment they can glimpse at its centre the red star high above, and on either side, washed away by the rain, a few slogans about the glory of work, and finally teetering to and fro among the huge potholes they turn into a larger bus yard situated between a few unspeakably wretched huts: the driver steps on the brake, the conductor opens the door and the vehicle, with a huge groaning sound, comes to a stop.

Stein and his companion don't even move, but when they see that the other travellers are lethargically beginning to gather up their things and, one after the other, getting off the bus, nothing remains but for them to do the same. They look over here, they look over there, but there is nothing even remotely resembling a mountain anywhere in sight, all around they see flat cornfields, and across from them a grimy concrete building: the driver and the conductor wordlessly pack up their things and leave the bus so quickly that they can barely catch up.

'This still isn't Jiuhuashan, is it' – they ask. 'When will the bus be leaving again?'

Neither the conductor nor the bus driver utters a single word, they don't even slow down, like people with some kind of urgent business: in one moment they have already disappeared into the building. Jiuhuashan – they try again, here with one traveller, there with another, but nobody answers. Jiuhuashan, they say to a few young men standing underneath the eaves of the building, but they too just look at them, then, sniggering, turn away in confusion. Then they notice a small group: there is something unusual about them, because suddenly they pick up their belongings and set off for the rear corner of the muddy yard: a few battered minivans are waiting there. Nothing betrays that they would be utilised for any purpose whatsoever, nonetheless there are one or two people sitting in each, and if they are not doing anything, if they are not giving any kind of sign of waiting for passengers, it's still as if the people surging towards them somehow know better – so it seems to the two Europeans that it would be best if they too joined the back of the small group, in other respects not too reassuring-looking, straining towards the minivans, and to try yet again:

'Jiuhuashan?'

A woman of about 60 looks back at them with a cheerful, friendly gaze, nods, and points at the battered vehicle.

'Jiuhuashan!'

The group immediately begins to talk to a man sitting behind the steering wheel of one of the minivans, but he just gazes indifferently ahead, as if he were completely alone in the universe. The people in the group, however, don't give up, they just keep on talking and talking and talking until the man slowly turns his head towards them, looks them up and down, then climbs out from behind the steering wheel with difficulty, and as if he wasn't really in the mood for this, with a surly expression, fiddles for a long time with the lock, then finally opens the door and the usual battle for seats begins, and although this time they encounter a considerable amount of difficulty, everyone behaves as if everything were perfectly normal, gazing ahead readily and confidently, until the man behind the steering wheel looks them up and down one by one as if, one would hope, he were counting them, then mutters something to the person sitting next to him, and starts up the motor.

On either side of the van there are two rows of seats – there are eight seats altogether – but there are fifteen people on the bus, so, compared to the large bus on which they had travelled up to this point, an even more impossible situation has presented itself: fifteen people and their packages to fit nine places. Nobody raises the question of what if, for example, another minivan from among at least the three others sitting in the yard would undertake the task of transporting the passengers, there is no grumbling, not one single ill-intentioned word is spoken – on the contrary, a kind of satisfaction can be felt in the air as they press up against one another just as much as they can, and if it seemed inconceivable at the beginning, within a minute everyone is inside and in their place, piled on top of one another, tightly pressed against each other – Stein and his companion are once again at the very back, and directly in front of them is the woman with the cheerful, friendly gaze, as well as someone else who is clearly travelling with her who looks also to be about 60, who are in the strictest sense of the word their neighbours, and the proximity of these two among the invariably none-too-reassuring faces is immediately comforting because, beyond the obvious reassurance of their presence they provide, on the one hand, a kind of guarantee that the direction in which the two foreigners wish to go is the correct one, and, on the other hand, they reinforce the belief that there will be something which they too will be able to understand in this country, operating amid opaque rules and regulations, as for example what is going on here, and what is the explanation here; because this is obviously a long-distance bus terminal, but in Nanjing nobody said anything about how the Nanjing buses come only this far, and then you have to get onto a smaller vehicle, if you wish to go further, as they wish to, and very much so; they sit silently, pressed up against the back seat, and they look ahead towards the driver to see if they are starting off yet, and in the meantime they feel more and more relieved, both Stein and his interpreter: look, they weren't lost after all, they weren't going in the wrong direction and the sacred mountain they are seeking, the hoped-for goal of their journey, Jiuhuashan, cannot be so far away now.

The road onto which they soon turn runs along a flat hillside, and is much worse than any other road upon which they have travelled so far. Actually it isn't even a road, just two travel-worn tracks in the mud, but the passengers don't seem to be in the least bit worried. Instead, when they are jolted around by an unavoidable pot-hole

E

and the bus throws all of them up against the roof, the response is loud laughter, when going along one of these indescribable tiny roads after a while the conditions become worse and nothing remains except a breathtakingly thin, serpentine strip, from which the wheels on the right side practically hang off, the people do not grow anxious, saying oh my god, what will happen, we're going to slip, and we're going to plummet into the abyss hardly visible in the ever-thickening fog, no, instead a kind of liveliness spreads from the front to the back, and from the back to the front, and the conversation starts up, and even Stein immediately realises that he is not preoccupied with the indisputable dangers and uncertainties, but with the two women pressed up and squatting in front of them, because after about ten minutes, as the passengers breathe into the bus and it begins to warm up, both of them push back their hoods onto their broad cloth coats and their shaven heads become visible – and already it can be seen that both of them have the same yellow travel bag, sewn from the same material, and nothing else – oh, Stein suddenly realises, they are pilgrims, and he looks at them, particularly at the one with the more cheerful gaze who was so friendly and helpful at the bus terminus, he examines her features, and joyfully determines that the gaze is not only friendly and cheerful, but also within it is a kind of simple grace, a naïve, innocent serenity, perpetually radiant, that is how she looks out of the window, that is how she observes the outburst of laughter at one huge jolt or another, that is how she looks back at him sometimes, at the Caucasian with that large nose – clearly amusing to her – that gaunt white man who is scrutinising the vehicle and those among whom he is travelling: who are these people in front of him, in these identical, long coats of broadcloth, with that identical yellow bag in their laps? Her companion is very different, Stein realises: she gazes forward with a serious, intelligent, thoughtful expression, as if she were examining the road to see if they are really going in the right direction in the drizzling rain, and despite her identical clothing and shaven skull it is suddenly clear that she is a completely different kind of person. He observes her delicate glasses, her elegant, cared-for hands, the evident pride and resolution in her posture, and he thinks that unlike the other one, she is most probably wealthy and educated, she seems a little colder, or more stern, more peremptory, more worldly – one thing that is certain, he decides, is that woman comes from modern China, the China that he, Stein, is trying to escape, so that, well, if they too are pilgrims, they are completely different from each other, and his attention keeps returning involuntarily to the more friendly of the two, betraying which one is most sympathetic to him, which of course is not so difficult, for in that naïve, serene, friendly creature there is something disarmingly worthy of love – he sits at the very back of the bus, he too looks at what can be seen from the road and the chasm among the shoulders and heads bouncing up and down, then he looks again at this serenity, at this forbearance, this innocence, and he thinks well, she seems like someone – even here, even in China,

E

where a traveller such as him can never be careful enough, according to prudent advice – to whom one would entrust everything.

He tries to make out the landscape outside as much as he can in a situation as difficult as this, because he can feel that they are headed upward, but for a while he sees more of the two dear female pilgrims than of the life-threatening, winding, serpentine road, plunged into ever thicker fog, he hears the engine straining, as the driver struggles with the gearbox, as he continually tries to force it into third gear when it can only go into second, the road is too steep, and the bends are too sharp, he brakes, second, third, and quickly back into second, they tilt this way, they tilt that way; the people in front of him press down on him with such force that at times Stein feels as if he himself is supporting the entire load, but he doesn't bother with this discomfort, he isn't interested in the difficulties, because now the lively cheerfulness has infected him and what if this is already Jiuhuashan, he thinks after a bend in the road, oh! he says loudly to the interpreter, maybe we are already in Jiuhuashan, maybe we are heading upward on Jiuhuashan – he sees that the passengers are taking out money, and passing it on forward to the driver, so they ask the friendly pilgrim how much, five yuan per person she says, the interpreter counts out 10 for both of them, puts it in the pilgrim's hand, gestures for her to pass it on forward, the high spirits are general, clearly the two foreigners are not the only ones who have made a long journey up to this point, and it can be tangibly felt that they are now in the last kilometres, it is almost certain now that they will arrive shortly, everyone will be up there very soon, and if they have no specific idea of who this everyone is – and it would be difficult, because it is hard to determine from the dark, wretched faces why they have come, if they are tourists, or if they came here to work, or if perhaps they live up here – it still occurs to Stein that the two women who look like pilgrims are not pilgrims, but nuns from one of the nunneries up there, my god, he tries to stoop so he can see something out of the tiny window of the minivan, so here he is in Jiuhuashan, and now, on the last part of the journey going upward: he thinks back to how they set off in Nanjing and the journey from Nanjing up to this point, he recalls how at the terminus they found the bus going here completely by chance, and it suddenly comes to mind how hopeless it was, indeed, the journey here ever and ever and ever more hopeless, as in a fairy tale, but at once he feels certain that he did the right thing, yes, the right thing in designating Jiuhuashan as the first goal of his journey, his planned quest for the detritus of Chinese classical culture, yes, precisely this abandoned Buddhist mountain: everyone tried to talk him out of coming here, just what are you thinking, what will you find there, his Chinese friends asked him, there's nothing there any more, nothing that you would hope for, no kind of hope at all, not least in Jiuhuashan, they noted disapprovingly, and just shook their heads; he however, precisely now in the perspective of this desolation, sees clearly that he *is on*

E

the right path, that he had to come here, exactly here on these muddy roads and these life-threatening serpentine bends, when some kind of movement starts up toward the front of the seats, and his ear is struck by a fragment of an angrier conversation, it is the driver, he can tell with his companion, it is the driver who is repeating something in a rage, pointing at them, of course they don't understand, it emerges only slowly, in the regional dialect, what he wants: it's the money, they should pass it over to him, he says, the 10 yuan, he throws back threateningly, and the others too explain and show that they, the two Caucasians, still haven't paid and the driver is ever more enraged, but now they are too, because of course they paid, the interpreter answers, they sent the money forward earlier, the interpreter looks at the serene-faced pilgrim: she does not confirm anything, but to their greatest surprise turns her head away, she does not intervene in the conversation which, because of the 10 yuan, is growing ever more ominous, they just keep repeating that they gave it to the female pilgrim, and the driver yells that their 10 yuan never made it over to him, and he steps on the brake, this is the last straw, everyone else has paid, the female pilgrim just sits there silently and stares out of the window with her unchanging serene gaze, this is impossible, the interpreter bursts out in rage, beginning to argue with the pilgrim that they certainly handed over – right into her hand! – the 10 yuan, at which point the female pilgrim says to the driver that she has no idea what money these foreigners are talking about, and at this they are struck dumb, Stein, horrified, tries to catch her gaze, the interpreter tries ever more furiously to force her to hand over the money, and it goes on like this for while, when suddenly two things happen: first, the companion of the female pilgrim, the more serious one, the less sympathetic one, says something softly to the other, and the other takes out the 10 yuan and passes it forward without a word; second, Stein comprehends that this pure naïveté – this innocent serenity, this sudden object of his confidence and affection – is a thief, she wanted to steal the 10 yuan, he realises, a realisation that comes with great difficulty simply because he doesn't want to believe it, but it did happen: the bus starts off again and in the ensuing silence – with the successful resolution of this affair the people sitting in front of them become quiet – he must grasp, he must recognise, he must reconcile himself to the fact that this Buddhist pilgrim or nun cheated him, and how! – for here she sits in the same serene tranquillity, her back turned towards him, and looking out of the window with the same innocent gaze as if nothing at all had happened, as if she hadn't stolen the money; she did, however, steal it, and that hurts the most, that she is a pilgrim, a nun, in this broad cloth coat, with a pilgrim's bag, en route towards the Buddha, and that she tried to cheat a defenceless foreigner – but they are very close to the goal, when as if at the touch of a magic wand the bus suddenly emerges from the fog, they can glimpse the peak of the mountain, and the sun is shining everywhere, it shines directly through the grimy windows of the minivan, every colour is sharp, deep, warm, and

E

everything is floating in the green, it's Jiuhuashan, says the interpreter reassuringly, and to get him out of this state, places a hand on his shoulder, yes, Jiuhuashan, he nods, but it's not so easy for him, he is still not able to recover from what just happened; out there, however, the sun is shining, they rattle alongside monks in yellow robes, yes, here they are, Stein grimly answers the interpreter, and then requests for something to be translated to the female pilgrim, because he has something to say to her – leave it, the interpreter tries to dissuade him – no, he insists, please translate this:

'So, how are you going to settle this with the Buddha? Those lousy 10 yuan? ARE YOU GOING TO SPLIT IT?'

Shush, the interpreter tries to quiet him down, and points towards the buildings amassed on the side of the mountain, and on the other side the breath-taking chasm, stop it, really, the interpreter nods in a forward direction; and already the first monastery buildings are visible, clearly this is the main street, teeming everywhere with monks, shops selling devotional objects and even lodgings – and they stop exactly here, exactly here they get out of the bus, the sun shines into their eyes, and completely blinded, they try to make out where they are, but there is just this sudden illumination and the sense that somewhere over there on the left there could be the mountain's steep slope and the famous peak, and about half a minute goes by until, as their eyes grow used to the light, suddenly they see the entire thing as one whole, and everywhere there are countless monasteries, they just stare at the buildings thickly woven across the side of the mountain, the wondrous yellow monastery walls and the green and the green everywhere, they gaze at the monks flocking around them curiously just as the monks look at them, then further on are the paths leading upward from the main street toward the monasteries – and everything is forgotten, he will try to figure out later, Stein decides, what was intended by this whole little petty theft, how to explain it, and in general: what did it mean, what was its significance, had he really misunderstood something, when suddenly the female pilgrim or nun with the serious face comes over to him, and in the friendliest possible manner explains to the interpreter – when she sees that between the two of them only he understands Chinese – that the entrance in front of which they are waiting is that of the lodgings, it is quite adequate, they can go inside, she shows them, this is not the case for all of the lodgings in Jiuhuashan, she warns them good-naturedly, not every one is... good, she leans her head to one side, but this one is, you can stay in this one, and so smiling, she waves farewell with a delicate movement and as if a little in excuse for the unpleasantness which they had to suffer just now because of her companion, she sets off on one of the paths with quick tiny steps, up into the heights, towards a monastery, in order to reach her companion, the guilty one, who, with a freshness belying her age, is already running up the steep path, and for a while they can still see that naïve, lovable, dear face which just shines and shines in this sharp pure sunlight, as she

E

turns to look at them now and again as if she wanted to show them, until she is finally swallowed up by the green of the path, that nothing, but nothing will ever wipe away that admired, illusory innocence from that face – ever.

E

POEMS

BY

KO UN

(*tr.* BROTHER ANTHONY OF TAIZÉ
& LEE SANG-WHA)

253

오슬로 역을 떠나면서
차창 밖
줄곧 동행하는 호수이셨네
강이 아닌 호수이셨네

그 길고 긴 호수
나의 길 가는 대로 따라오셨네

끝내 릴레함메르
호수 건너 저 세상
호수 건너 이 세상
거기까지도 따라오셨네

꽃 많이 받고
사진 많이 찍고
질문 여러 개에 대답한 뒤
거기까지 함께 온 호수
아니
혼자서 더 가려는 호수에
절하러 나가니

하늘 전체의 낙조들
그 호수가 다 맞이하여
내 아내한테 주셨네
나한테 주셨네

어디다 눈길 줄 수 없고
어디다 말을 걸 수 없는 기쁨
무능의 기쁨으로
죽은 벗을 그리워할 때

호수는 온 길로 느리게 느릿하게 돌아가셨네

253

After we left Oslo station
the lake kept accompanying us
outside of the window.
It was a lake, not a river.

That long, long lake
kept following us on our way.

It eventually followed us
to Lillehammer, that city,
that place across the lake,
this place across the lake.

After receiving many bunches of flowers,
being photographed many times,
answering a number of questions,
I went out to salute the lake
that had accompanied us,
that would now go farther on its own.

Then, the lake greeted
all the glowing of the whole twilight sky,
gave it to my wife
and to me.

When I missed a dead friend
with a joy such that I knew not where to look,
what to say,
with that incompetent joy,

The lake went back slowly, leisurely the way it had come.

신호덕이

이른 봄 배는 고픈데
똥거름 냄새 푸짐하구나
보리밭 머리
뚝새 냉이 벌금자리 캐는 호덕이
호덕이 등짝에 내려올 햇볕
구름이 가렸구나

하늘 속
하늘의 구름 속 종달새
내려다 보니
저 아래 호덕이 저 혼자 배고프며 노래하고 노래 듣누나

달도 하나 해도 하나 사랑도 하나......

Shin Ho-deok

In early spring the stomach's empty;
but how full the stench of night soil is!
At the edge of the barley field
Ho-deok is grubbing up early spring greens.
Look how a cloud is blocking the sunlight
to keep it from beating on Ho-deok's back.

The skylark up in the sky
up in the clouds in the sky
looks down and listens
while down below Ho-deok all alone, hungry, sings.

'The moon is one, the sun is one, and love is one . . .'

그 형제

형 김동삼이 고향을 떠났다
뜨르르한 고대광실
뜨르르한 전답 다 두고
잃어버린 나라 찾아야 한다고
고향의 밤을 떠났다
아우 김동만도
술 한 잔 없이
형의 뒤를 따라 고향을 떠났다

만주벌판 눈보라 속

하루 백리 백오십리를 걸었다
담요 한 장 말아
어깨에 메고
헤진 여름신발에 동여매고 걸었다

한 푼 주고 사 먹는
만주 전병 한 끼로 끼니를 때우며
하루 백리 백오십리를 걸었다

서간도
북간도 벌판과 산기슭을 걷고 걸었다
걸어가다

마적떼 만나면 숨고
산짐승 만나면
불 놓아 쫓으며 걸었다

걸어가다 동포를 만나면
교육결사
군사결사
생활결사 경학사 설립을 호소했다

이도구에서
삼도구에서
두도구에서
그들 형제 내내 함께였다
다른 동지도 함께였다

아직 옛 시대 사색당파 남아있었다
지역당파
무슨 당파
무슨 당파 갈라져 있었다
그런 동포 만나
하나의 나라 외치며
목 타는 입 안에 고드름을 녹였다

아우 김동만의 입에서
어쩌다 한 마디가 나와버렸다
어머니 !

형 김동삼이 아우를 돌아다보았다

Two Brothers

The elder brother, Kim Dong–sam, left home.
Abandoning their impressive mansion,
their wide–spreading fields,
he left home by night
saying he had to regain the nation they'd lost.
His younger brother, Kim Dong–man,
without taking so much as a single drink,
left home, following his elder brother.

Up in the snow–swept Manchurian plains

they walked thirty, forty miles a day.
One folded blanket
tied across their shoulders
their battered summer shoes bound with string, they walked on.

Making do with one meal a day
of Manchurian pancakes, bought for a penny,
they walked thirty or forty miles a day.

They walked and walked
across the plains and the hills of West Kanto and North Kanto.

On they walked,
hiding if they encountered bands of brigands,
lighting a fire if they encountered wild animals.
If they met fellow–countrymen along the way
they would call for the establishment
of educational associations
military associations
life associations, study associations.

In Erh-tao-kou,
in San-tao-kou,
in T'ou-tao-kou
those brothers were together all the time
with other comrades too.

There were still remains of the Four Factions of Korea's ancient times,
regional factions,
this faction
and that faction, all living divided.
When they met such fellow-countrymen
they would cry out: We are all one nation!
as they sucked icicles in thirsty mouths.

Once a single word escaped from
the lips of the young Kim Dong-man:
'Mother!'
His elder brother, Kim Dong-sam, rounded on him.

180

귀신고래 솟듯
귀신고래 잠기듯
파도에 대하여 세련될지어니
파도 밑에 대하여
숙련될지어니

이번에는 뭍의 의지일지어니

캠포라나무는
가지가 아닌
줄기가 몇십개씩 뻗어나간다
남아프리카공화국 케이프타운쯤
그곳 커스텐보쉬쯤

결코 외줄기로 서지 않는 것

옛 부시맨은 사나모뭄나무라 했던 나무
그 캠포라 줄기들 밑
나무와 사람이 서로 믿는다
네슨 만델라가 서서 중얼거린다
'나는 야생 속에 있을 때
가장 행복하다' 라고

뒷날 누가 그 자리에 서서 댓글을 단다
'나는 누가 있던 곳에 있을 때
가장 행복하다'라고

두 녀석 다
어릴 적 젖먹이 적으로부터 멀리도 와서
결코 외줄기가 아닌
세월 속 여러 줄기들의 하나하나일지어니

180

We should be skilled with waves,
be sophisticated
about what is beneath the waves
as gray whales soar up,
as gray whales sink down.

Now we should be the will of the dry land.

Camphor trees
spread dozens of trunks
that are not branches,
around Cape Town, South Africa,
out there, near Kirstenbosch,

never standing as a single trunk.

The ancient bushmen called it the cinnamomum tree,
and beneath the trunks of those camphor trees
trees and humans trust one another.
Nelson Mandela stands murmuring:
'I am happiest
when I'm in the wild.'

Later, someone stood there, adding:
'I am happiest
when I am in a place where someone has been.'

Both fellows
have come a long way from the time when they were nursing babies
and become one among multiple trunks,
never a single, independent trunk.

TRANSLATION IN
THE FIRST PERSON

BY

KATE BRIGGS

IT IS 1 JUNE 2015 and I am standing outside no. 11 rue Servandoni in Paris's sixth arrondissement. I have lived in this city, on and off, for over ten years. I've walked in and through the Jardin de Luxembourg many times, likewise the loop around Place Saint-Sulpice (I can see now how the rue Servandoni serves as a corridor between the two). But it so happens, I realise, that I've never walked down this particular street before. Now that I'm here, I'm wondering why it has never, not once, occurred to me to seek this building out: the building where Roland Barthes lived for twenty years, from 1960 to 1980, in an apartment on the sixth floor.

I'm standing outside no. 11, the street is empty, the sun is warm and I'm trying hard to feel something of the curiosity – what Barthes would call a biographical curiosity, of the kind that would unexpectedly fire him up late in life – that might have prompted me to do so.

I try imagining a body. For instance, leaning some of its weight against one of the heavy double doors, pushing it open, stepping inside and climbing the stairs marked B.

Or a forefinger punching out the building code: once, twice, several times a day, over the space of twenty years.

But the thing is: I'm finding it difficult. Much easier to summon are the characters that Alexandre Dumas has live next door. Here is D'Artagnan, the new Musketeer, defending Constance with clashing swords; here are the two of them creeping along this very street at dusk; here are the neighbours who close their shutters and all go to bed early.

It's not that I am uncurious about the life Barthes lived upstairs. I know that's not it, because, really, I'm fascinated.

It's more that what I am most *urgently* interested in – what I came here today, hot and self-conscious on the bus, especially to consider – is my own pavement position.

It is 1 December 1976 and Barthes is looking out of the window. He sees a woman walking with her child on the street below.

In his notes he writes her like this: she is holding the kid by the hand, walking and pushing the empty buggy out ahead.

Buggy, pushchair: these were my original British-English translations of *poussette.*

E

But the words mean different things to an American reader, so I learn. Because of this, they are rejected by the copy-editor in favour of *stroller*.

The woman is walking steadily, purposively, at her own pace. The child, meanwhile, is being pulled along. Or dragged. She is dragging him, notes Barthes: tugging at his arm, forcing him to run to keep up. Like an animal. Or more hyperbolically still: like one of Sade's victims being whipped. Here is the woman walking, steadily and purposively at her own pace, seemingly unaware that her child's walking rhythm is different. Barthes is – what? Dismayed, indignant, outraged. He writes, with emphasis: *And she's his mother!*

I have often thought of this woman. More specifically, I've often thought of her as I've walked with my own children, in a nearby but quite different neighbourhood of Paris, with the work of translating Barthes's sentences agitating at my brain. Walking and doing exactly as he describes: tugging at my sons, pushing an empty buggy, striding (not strolling) ahead, failing – sometimes even making a point of refusing – to calibrate my pace with theirs. Clearly, or so it has always seemed to me, there's something excessive to the point of comical about Barthes's instant outrage. Maybe they were late? Maybe she just wanted to get home? Maybe she was thinking about something else? Maybe she was tired?

Still, I can see his point. For Barthes, briefly caught by this dynamic of mother and child are the central concerns of the lecture course he was preparing at the time. And I register how the point is being made. I know it's important that the scene should have been glimpsed from a window, appearing bright and striking against the background of other, more or less absorbing, daily activities. In a lecture course where the ethical is made explicitly a matter of everyday social interactions and relations, Barthes would use the walking woman to describe how power can appear as rhythmic incompatibility. In other words, how power gets exercised and felt in the imposition of one rhythm on another.

The pavement directly outside Barthes's apartment building is reasonably wide. Wide enough for a woman, empty buggy and child. But it narrows to something more like a ledge as the street inclines towards the park. Sooner or later, she would have had to walk in the road, negotiating the curb and the parked cars with her empty buggy and her small son. If this, indeed, is where he saw her. The sixth floor has a deep balcony. Would Barthes have had a clear view of the street below? Probably not. Perhaps he was looking out of his office at the Collège de France? Did he have an office there? Did it have a window? I could find out. I could ask his biographers, his editors, those

E

who knew him. I could stand on the rue Saint-Jacques instead, conscientious in my investigation of the *bad mother* (as she's described in the preface to the French edition).

I don't, though. Because what concerns me is exactly this: the not-knowing, the distance. I have never been inside, *with* Barthes, as he drafted his lecture courses for the first time. I was born two years after the first course was conceived. But I have *been with* the written and recorded Barthes – the notes and the voice – in the thoroughly mediated sense of *being-with* that is produced in and by the action of writing his sentences and bits of sentences again.

A strange action. The translator Helen Lowe-Porter would call it *a little art*. But one that is still, even so, and somehow as a consequence, productive of its own kind of knowledge, and its own peculiarly detached proximity. Like reading through a microscope?

I think of a note that Walter Benjamin made on his experience of translating Proust. Something like: *I am so close to the prose now that I can no longer see the details*. A note I have been thinking about for years. Because it seems to me that translation does exactly this: mess up the relation between the part and the whole, making the near distend so far into the far that another reader's relative distance starts looking like closeness. But I can no longer remember where I read it.

All of a sudden I *wanted* to do this: to stand below what was once Barthes's window. And so here I am: looking up and failing to imagine him looking out, contemplating what it is to be oddly together and wholly at odds with another writing body writing at another time, and thinking once again of the walking woman whose path, some forty years ago, happened to cross his line of sight. I wanted to see if I could occupy that unknown woman's place in his notes in order to expand it. To inhabit this scene of looking and being looked at in order to rewrite it for my own purposes, as a way of taking some bodily measure of my own relation to – my own nearly felt distance from – the late life and work of Roland Barthes.

And also to see whether, in the process, I might add to, or displace, some of the meanings the walking woman has been assigned.

She is not only the bad mother, the briefly glimpsed, indifferent regulator of rhythms.

She is now, also, me: the as yet unseen translator-to-come. I rename her. Like that

E

moment in *The Three Musketeers* when Aramis, disguised a priest, renames the meat dish they'll all be having for Friday night dinner: 'I baptise you: Carp!'

It sounds presumptuous, I know.

Still. It is here, in the unlikely conjunction of (for example) Barthes and me, that I think an account of the work of translation should begin.

It is 1921 and the publisher Alfred A. Knopf has acquired the exclusive translation rights to publish Thomas Mann's works in English. The translator he eventually commissions, four years later, is Helen Tracy Lowe-Porter. Then aged 44, she would work on the translations of Mann's works for the next twenty five years, stopping only in her late sixties, partly because of ill health and partly to pursue, or to resume, her own literary projects (poems, a play). Lowe-Porter's translations would be extraordinarily successful: fast-selling and popular with the reading public. New versions of Mann's works have appeared in the years since Knopf's claim on the rights expired, but Lowe-Porter's work is still everywhere in print.

It is 1995 and the scholar Tim Buck publishes an article in the *Times Literary Supplement*. It would be a devastating and, in the small circles of translation scholarship, now notorious indictment of Lowe-Porter's translations. Comparing a random sample of passages from *Buddenbrooks* in Mann's original German with the English translation, Buck lists mistake after mistake after mistake. Errors of lexis, syntax and tense; unexplained omissions; unjustified re-phrasings. At times, says Buck, Lowe-Porter looks like a *bungling amateur*, with a strikingly inadequate knowledge of German. Worse, an amateur with *an inflated sense of her own importance* – either wholly ignorant of her own limitations, or unwilling to acknowledge them. Lowe-Porter was not Mann's chosen translator, Buck tells us. He wanted someone with better German. Not only was her German poor, look at her English: *ungainly, unidiomatic, and at times incomprehensible.* She *pressed* for the *honour* of translating Mann; not relenting until *the prize of being Mann's translator was hers.* She was *hungry* for the cultural capital that Buck is sure that she felt sure would come her way via the long-term association of her name with his. How could this have happened? Extrapolating, the main complaint of the article seems to come down to this. Was no one checking? Was no one in charge? How is it possible that the English Mann and, by implication, the whole great machine of literary history, should have been determined in this way – so contingently, so unthinkingly, by the vagaries of one woman's writing desire?

E

Following the article's publication came a small rush of letters to the editor. Lawrence Venuti wrote in, strongly objecting to the *typical academic condescension* toward translators and translation he detected in Buck's article, and tried building a defense of Lowe–Porter's mistakes out of the general point that standards for what makes a good translation change. There exists a tacit aesthetics of translation; one that, like all aesthetic traditions, is necessarily of its time. David Luke, whose 1988 translation of Mann's 'Death in Venice' Buck had praised (*a model translation: faithful to the original, yet fluent*) replied with new evidence of still more mistakes, and still more condescension. You can't blame Mann's complex sentences for this, he argued, or changes in what counts for accuracy in translation. No, what we are dealing with here is failure. Just look at her *schoolboy howlers!* Venuti came back with another letter; Luke replied again. Eventually, Lowe–Porter's daughters wrote in with an account of how their late mother conceived of her work.

A perverse pleasure, she called it.

Offering its own experience of creative authorship.

Look to the whole, the daughters asked.

And note the promise she lived by: she would not send her translations to the publisher unless *she felt as though she had written the books herself.*

Amateur translator.

(What would it take, what would it mean, I wonder, to become *an expert?*)

In circuitous pursuit of original creation.

Would–be writer who refuses to let go of her translations until she feels she has written the books herself.

This is the position I am interested in. It is the one I want to think and write out from. Because there are perverse pleasures to be had in the work of translation. There is romance: intensely ambivalent affairs between translators and the works they have been tasked with making again – complicated feelings that can extend to the body of the body that made them first. *Leibe Tommy* is how, in her letters, Helen Lowe–Porter would come to address the writer whose writing she had been writing for some twenty years. *Dearest Gide* is how Dorothy Bussy, Gide's devoted translator, would

E

begin some of hers. There is audacity and appropriation, together with drawn-out and difficult, long-term learning. There is something like speculative simulation: all translations are propositions, I think, working their way outward from an originating and peculiarly novelistic *as if*. An enabling fiction that the translator sets down before she begins, that she must set down as a condition of her beginning. (*Let's say that she wrote the books herself!*) There are, also, these great tracts of life-time, of time spent with someone else's work: translation as a daily practice that is enabled by and in a fundamental sense dependent upon distance, difference, and implausibility.

It is 1978 and Barthes is delivering a lecture titled with a sentence: *Longtemps je me suis couché de bonne heure*, the opening line of *A LA RECHERCHE DU TEMPS PERDU*. Should we take this to mean that the lecture would be *on* Proust? Yes and no. The actual topic would be (if you will, asks Barthes, if you'll indulge me on this): Proust and me. Sounds presumptuous, I know. Nietzsche spared no irony on the Germans' use of that conjunction. Schopenhauer *and* Hartmann, he would jeer. *Really?* Proust and me, says Barthes, sounds even worse (the link it makes, the connection it presumes, is even bolder). And yet. Paradoxically, all the presumption falls away the moment it is the subject who's speaking for himself, from the moment that it is clearly Barthes who's speaking, and not some observer. In making this association between himself and Proust, putting them both on the same level in this way, the point is not to *compare* himself to a great writer, but rather to affirm, in a very different manner, that *he identifies with him*: confusion of *practice*, not of value. Let me explain, says Barthes: in figurative literature, in the novel, for example, it seems true to say that we identify with one of the characters represented (I mean, intermittently, for stretches of our reading if not throughout). This projection, I believe, is one of the animating forces, the wellsprings of literature; but in some marginal cases, in the case, for example, of the reader who has writerly ambitions of his own, the reading subject no longer identifies exclusively with one or other of the characters represented. He also, and principally, identifies with the author of the book he is reading, for the reason that the author must have wanted to write this work and has clearly succeeded. Now, Proust is the privileged site of this peculiar form of identification, since *IN SEARCH OF LOST TIME* is the narrative of a desire to write: I'm not identifying with the prestigious author of a monumental work of literature, I'm identifying with the writer-as-*labourer* – now tormented, now exalted, but in all events *modest* –

I –

Which 'I' now? Barthes or me? –

E

Me: the translator (mother/walker/would-be writer) standing on the pavement out-side.

I *pressed* for the honour of translating Barthes's lecture notes – especially the notes for a lecture course on the novel, that public acting-out of a private desire to write. Notes for a lecture course that I had, inappropriately, fallen in love with. I think that's the quickest way of describing it.

Why these bits of writing and not others? It's a puzzle that Barthes wonders around in his notes: Why, for him, is it Proust's IN SEARCH OF LOST TIME? Why is it ANNA KARENINA and not WAR AND PEACE? Why, across the differentiated corpus of ap-parently the same author, is it for me the late, oddly provisional works (the lectures, not the books) and not the others?

Or to put it another way: What are the chances of our attachments?

Thomas Mann's preferred translator either fell or jumped out of a window. In the weeks that followed, his publishers got back in touch with Helen Lowe-Porter.

I think of all the unlikely writer-translator pairs. And then consider why, of all the powerful forces that decide these pairings, haphazardly determining whose name will be linked with whose, I should be most interested in the *preferences* of the indi-vidual translator.

I *like*: cinnamon, marzipan, lavender, Pollock, Twombly, ice-cold beer, the smell of new-cut hay.

I *don't like*: the afternoons, geraniums, women in trousers. Who cares? asks Barthes, after writing his list of likes and dislikes out like a poem. All of this is of absolutely no consequence to anyone whatsoever. It is all apparently meaningless. And yet, what it means – or, more literally – what it *wants to say* is: *my body is not the same as yours*.

The risk that all of this will read like an apology for the lady translator, picking her projects, subject only to her own inclinations.

I worry about this for all of two minutes, before it strikes me, with great, sud-den clarity: So what? She translated too. Helen Lowe-Porter: 'I translated BUDDENBROOKS in the intervals of rocking the cradle (not quite single-handed, for I had a little maid at £40 an hour).' Perhaps we could agree that to the extent that we experience our labour as unalienated, to the extent that for whatever complex set of reasons and life circumstances we can afford or find it incumbent upon ourselves to work slowly and for relatively little pay, to the extent that the work we do can be qualified as *literary*, we are all lady translators.

It is December in the mid-1970s and Barthes looks out of his window to see a walking woman, a mother and her child, who will unknowingly become the central, crystallising image for a lecture course titled *HOW TO LIVE TOGETHER*.

In the new scene I am staging, it is summer 2015, the woman is a translator, her kids are at school and here she is standing on the pavement looking back up, thinking now about what Barthes really meant by *together*. Because regardless of the instant outrage at the mother who failed, so strikingly, to accommodate the pace of her child, it is not clear that togetherness, for Barthes, has anything to do with being in sync.

The book *ROLAND BARTHES*, written by Roland Barthes, is published in French in 1975. It features a photograph of the author as a toddler at the seaside. He is carrying a tiny bucket and wearing a large hat. Near it is written: *Contemporaries? I had just started walking, Proust was still alive, and finishing LA RECHERCHE*. In the lecture course he would start drafting a year later, Barthes asks the question again: Who are my contemporaries? With whom do I live? The calendar, telling only of the forward march of chronological time, is of little help. The way it brackets together work produced in the same set of years, as if a shared historical context were the condition, or the guarantor, of a relationship. The way it holds other, more distantly dated relations apart. There is a kind of fold, a kink, in the very contemporary, says Barthes: an untimeliness. Like the suddenly urgent topicality of an obscure essay on the monasteries of Mount Athos happened upon in the mid- to late 1970s. An essay whose strangely beautiful key word – *idiorrhythmy* – would open out onto questions of rhythm and power, the socialisation of time and the temporalisation of space, the possible forms of small-scale living together in literature and in life. Or the striking contemporaneity of Barthes's lecture notes in the eyes of their English-speaking readers. That is, when they're finally made available for reading in 2012, some forty-odd years after the fact. Or the dates I have been writing out here, plotting them on a line while at the same time wanting to show how the force of reading and identification turns the line into a thread to make loops, circles and tie knots with. For Barthes, it would appear that being-*productively*-with actually requires a measure of being-at-odds.

Something like delay.

E

Which is rhythm, as he notes here and elsewhere.

In matters of writing and reading and therefore, also, in matters of what matters to writers and readers – what pertains to their present moment, what is given to them to read in their own languages so that it is even possible for them to be struck by – the translator is an agent of delay.

That is to say, of spacing.

Not *now*. Not right now. At once, on the spot, as it happens.

But something more like

now

Isn't that what Benjamin says? A translation comes after the original. The point being: even when it doesn't. This is its circumstance. And everything, all the complication of its standing and its relations, unspools from there.

An agent of spacing and of *placing*. Unexpectedly seating *him* next to *her* and *her* next to *him* around this moment's table. Encouraging the conversations, enabling the arguments and the affinities. Whatever gets newly published in English translation this year will have little to do with the timings of the original productions. There will have been no real system to it. More like the arrangements of read and half-read and freshly returned books that sometimes get curated on library sorting trolleys.

The silent masters of culture, Maurice Blanchot called us.

Yeah, yeah, I think to myself, turning away from the sixth floor, preparing to go home now. I don't feel especially masterful. But I do feel less silent. I want to speak about this strange activity that has absorbed so many of my days. Although, to be clear: *not that many.* Not that many on the Helen Lowe–Porter or Dorothy Bussy scale of things. I want, even so, to make some provisional claim on the authority to write about the work of translation, about how it happens and about why, of all the things I might also want to do, I – and many others – should keep wanting to do this.

I make my way up the rue Servandoni, heading towards the bus-stop at the edge of the park. As the street inclines and the space for pedestrians narrows, I find myself walking as one of my children might: lolloping unevenly along, making a game out

E

of putting one foot up on what's now no more than a curb and the other in the gutter, apparently determined to maintain, at least for as long as the design of the ancient street will allow it, some kind of purchase on this (let's call it *my*?) strip of tapering pavement.

NOTES

what Barthes would call a biographical curiosity: when I was an undergraduate in the mid- to late Nineties, the only bit of Barthes on our lit theory reading list was 'The Death of the Author' (1967; translated by Richard Howard). On 19 January 1980, Barthes gave a lecture on 'The Return of the Author', which described his newfound curiosity about the life that produces the work. He had changed his mind, he had moved on, the focus of his interests had shifted. I'm not in the same place, he said; I'm not still there, awaiting you, immobile in my positions of some twenty years ago (I'm not where you expect me to be). Roland Barthes, *THE PREPARATION OF THE NOVEL*, trans. Kate Briggs (New York: Columbia University Press, 2011) pp. 207–215.

the characters that Alexandre Dumas has live next door: the rue Servandoni, formerly the rue des Fossoyeurs, has its own Wikipedia page. In *THE THREE MUSKETEERS* D'Artagnan lives at no. 7, which was renumbered and renamed no. 12 rue Servandoni in 1806.

In his notes he writes her like this: in the notes for the first lecture course that Barthes delivered at the Collège de France following his appointment as Chair of Literary Semiology. *HOW TO LIVE TOGETHER: NOVELISTIC SIMULATIONS OF SOME EVERYDAY SPACES*, trans. Kate Briggs (New York: Columbia University Press, 2013), p. 9.

Like the scene in THE THREE MUSKETEERS: Barthes quotes the line 'I baptise you Carp!' in his lecture course on the novel, as a way of claiming (and even making a pedagogical principle out of) the right to speak of 'his' haiku; that is, from the vantage point of his own particular, subjective relation to haiku, which he reads in French translation, having no reading knowledge of Japanese.

The translator he commissioned was Helen Tracy Lowe-Porter: for further detail on the circumstances of H. T. Lowe-Porter's commission see John C. Thirlwall's *IN ANOTHER LANGUAGE: A RECORD OF THE THIRTY YEAR RELATIONSHIP BETWEEN THOMAS MANN AND HIS ENGLISH TRANSLATOR, HELEN TRACY LOWE-PORTER*

(New York: Alfred A. Knopf, 1966). Also, David Morton's more recent, balanced account of her work which emphasises, as I want to here, the haphazardness of it all: THOMAS MANN IN ENGLISH: A STUDY IN LITERARY TRANSLATION (London: Bloomsbury, 2013).

In 1995 the scholar Tim Buck published an article in the TIMES LITERARY SUPPLEMENT: 'Neither the letter nor the spirit: Why most English translations of Thomas Mann are so inadequate', TIMES LITERARY SUPPLEMENT, 13 October 1995. Buck published variations on this article in THE CAMBRIDGE COMPANION TO THOMAS MANN edited by Ritchie Robertson (Cambridge: Cambridge University Press, 2002) and ENCYCLOPEDIA OF LITERARY TRANSLATION INTO ENGLISH VOL. 2. M–Z, edited by Olive Classe (London and Chicago: Fitzroy Dearborn Publishers, 2000). I am quoting from the three sources here. Laurence Venuti's letters to the editor were published on 24 November and 22 December 1995; David Luke's replies on 8 and 29 December 1995. The letter from Lowe–Porter's surviving daughters was published on 19 January 1996. The lines about perverse pleasure and the promise she made herself ('of never sending a translation to the publisher unless I felt I had written the book myself') come, respectively, from Lowe–Porter's letters and her essay 'On Translating Thomas Mann', published in Thirlwall's *In* ANOTHER LANGUAGE.

It is 1978 and Barthes is delivering a lecture: This lecture was translated by Richard Howard and included in THE RUSTLE OF LANGUAGE, trans. Richard Howard (Berkeley: University of California Press, 1989). Here I am working from and slightly modifying Howard's translation.

I like: cinnamon, marzipan, lavender: The full lists are in ROLAND BARTHES BY ROLAND BARTHES, trans. Richard Howard (New York: Hill and Wang, 2010).

I translated BUDDENBROOKS *in the intervals of rocking the cradle*: 'On Translating Thomas Mann', *In* ANOTHER LANGUAGE.

Contemporaries?: The question is asked again in HOW TO LIVE TOGETHER.

Which is rhythm: The formulation 'rhythm is delay' comes from Barthes's reading of CONVERSATIONS AVEC PABLO CASALS (Paris: Albin Michel, 1955). It appears in ROLAND BARTHES BY ROLAND BARTHES, in HOW TO LIVE TOGETHER, p. 35, and in THE NEUTRAL, his lecture course of the following year, translated by Rosalind E. Krauss and Denis Hollier (New York: Columbia University Press, 2005).

Isn't that what Benjamin says?: in 'The Task of the Translator' (1923), trans. Harry Zohn in ILLUMINATIONS (London: Pimlico, 1999).

The silent masters of culture: The line is in fact 'the hidden masters of culture'; it is 'our recognition' of translators' 'zeal' that 'remains silent'. 'Translating', FRIENDSHIP, trans. Elizabeth Rottenberg (Stanford: Stanford University Press, 1997).

SPONSORS

Rudolf Stingel

04 November – 18 December 2015
Tuesday – Saturday 11–6

Sadie Coles HQ
1 Davies Street London W1K 3DB
62 Kingly Street London W1B 5QN

www.sadiecoles.com

Sadie Coles   HQ

MICHAEL KREBBER
SEPTEMBER – OCTOBER

LIAM GILLICK
OCTOBER – NOVEMBER

HANNAH STARKEY
DECEMBER – JANUARY

MAUREEN PALEY. 21 HERALD STREET, LONDON E2 6JT +44 (0)20 7729 4112 INFO@MAUREENPALEY.COM WWW.MAUREENPALEY.COM

THE ICE PLANT www.theiceplant.cc

About Time

October 2015 - January 2016

About Time is a satellite programme of contemporary art to coincide with the launch of British Art Show 8. This city-wide initiative features commissioned artworks, texts and events which aim to highlight the work of artists, cultural producers and curatorial projects based in Leeds, alongside their international peers.

About Time is curated by a consortium of Leeds-based contemporary art initiatives led by Mexico, Pavilion and SPUR. It is supported by Arts Council England and Leeds Inspired.

www.about-time.org

OHWOW

Torey Thornton
Be Right Back, and Left, 2015
Metallic paint, acrylic and foam core on wood panel
96 x 82 inches / 243.8 x 208.3 cm

www.oh-wow.com

Fitzcarraldo Editions congratulates Svetlana Alexievich on winning the 2015 Nobel Prize in Literature. Her next book, *Second-Hand Time*, is forthcoming in May 2016 in Bela Shayevich's translation.

Fitzcarraldo Editions

www.fitzcarraldoedtions.com

APPENDIX

KATE BRIGGS is a writer and translator. She teaches at the American University of Paris and the Piet Zwart Institute, Rotterdam. 'Translation in the First Person' is an excerpt from *THIS LITTLE ART*, a book in progress about the practice of translation.

LUKE BROWN's debut novel *MY BIGGEST LIE* was published last year by Canongate. His piece in this issue is the beginning of a new novel.

ANNE CARSON was born in Canada and teaches Ancient Greek for a living.

MAYLIS DE KERANGAL spent her childhood in Le Havre, France. Her novel *BIRTH OF A BRIDGE* (Talon Books, 2014) was the winner of the Prix Franz Hessel and Prix Médicis in 2010. Her novella *TANGENTE VERS L'EST* (Verticales, 2012) was the winner of the 2012 Prix Landerneau. In 2014, her fifth novel, *RÉPARER LES VIVANTS* (Verticales, 2014), was published to wide acclaim, winning the Grand Prix RTL–Lire award and the student choice novel of the year from France Culture and Télèrama. *MEND THE LIVING*, its English translation excerpted here, is published in February 2016 by MacLehose Press (UK), FSG (USA), and Talon Books (Canada).

BRIAN DILLON's books include *THE GREAT EXPLOSION* (Penguin, 2015), *OBJECTS IN THIS MIRROR: ESSAYS* (Sternberg Press, 2014), *SANCTUARY* (Sternberg Press, 2011), *TORMENTED HOPE: NINE HYPOCHONDRIAC LIVES* (Penguin, 2009) and *IN THE DARK ROOM* (Penguin, 2005). He is UK editor of *CABINET* magazine, and reader in critical writing at the Royal College of Art. His next book, *ESSAYISM*, will be published by Fitzcarraldo Editions in 2016.

LAUREN ELKIN is the author of *FLÂNEUSE: ESSAYS IN WANDERING* (Chatto & Windus, July 2016). She is an award-winning novelist (*UNE ANNÉE À VENISE*, Editions Héloïse d'Ormesson) and the co-author of *THE END OF OULIPO? AN ATTEMPT TO EXHAUST A MOVEMENT* (with Scott Esposito, Zero Books). Her writing on literature and art has appeared in the *NEW YORK TIMES BOOK REVIEW*, the *TIMES LITERARY SUPPLEMENT*, *BOOKFORUM*, *FRIEZE*, and many other publications. She is a lecturer in English and Comparative Literature at the American University of Paris.

LUCY GREAVES translates from Spanish, Portuguese and French. She won the 2013 Harvill Secker Young Translators' Prize and in 2014 was Translator in Residence at the Free Word Centre in London. Her work has appeared in *GRANTA* and the *GUARDIAN*, among others, and she is currently translating María Angélica Bosco's *LA MUERTE BAJA EN EL ASCENSOR* which will be published by Pushkin Press. She lives in Bristol.

JENNIFER HODGSON is a writer and an academic. She is currently writing a book about the 1960s experimental novelist Ann Quin, and editing a collection of Quin's unpublished short stories.

NAVINE G. KHAN-DOSSOS studied History of Art at Cambridge University, Arabic at Kuwait University, Islamic Art at the Prince's School of Traditional Art, and completed her MA in Fine Art at Chelsea College of Art & Design. She was a participant at the Van Eyck Academie in Maastricht, and has taken part in residencies with the A.M. Qattan Foundation, Leighton House Museum, and the Delfina Foundation. She is also known as Vanessa Hodgkinson.

ANNETTE KELM (born 1975 in Stuttgart, Germany) lives and works in Berlin. Her work has been presented in solo exhibitions at international institutions, including Espace LouisVuitton, Munich and Kölnischer Kunstverein (2014), Presentation House Gallery, Vancouver (2012), Bonner Kunstverein (2011), Art Institute for Contemporary Art, Berlin (2009), Kunsthalle Zurich (2009) and CCA Wattis Institute, San Francisco (2008). In addition, Annette Kelm's works were featured in numerous group exhibitions, most recently at MoMA, New York (2013) and Frankfurter Kunstverein (2013). In 2012 she participated in the 12th Istanbul Biennial and in 2011 in the 54th Venice Biennial. She will have a solo show at the Museum of Contemporary Art in Detroit, curated by Jens Hoffman, in 2016.

CALEB KLACES is the author of BOTTLED AIR (Eyewear Publishing, 2013). 'Inter Alia' is the second part of a three-part poem. The first part, 'Genit—', was published in THE WHITE REVIEW NO.12 and reprinted in BEST BRITISH POETRY 2015.

LÁSZLÓ KRASZNAHORKAI was born in Gyula, Hungary, in 1954. He worked for some years as an editor until 1984, when he became a freelance writer. He now lives in reclusiveness in the hills of Szentlászló. He has written five novels and won numerous prizes, including the 2015 Man Booker International Prize, and the 2013 Best Translated Book Award in Fiction for SATANTANGO (New Directions, 2012). In 1993, he won the Best Book of the Year Award in Germany for THE MELANCHOLY OF RESISTANCE (New Directions, 2002). This piece is an extract from DESTRUCTION AND SORROW BENEATH THE HEAVENS, which will be published by Seagull Books in January 2016.

ALICJA KWADE (born 1979 in Katowice, Poland) lives and works in Berlin, where she studied at the Universität der Künste from 1999 to 2005. Recent solo exhibitions include Haus am Waldsee, Berlin (2015), Public Art Fund, New York (2015), Kunsthalle Mannheim (2015), Kunsthalle Nurnberg (2015), Kunsthalle Schirn in Frankfurt am Main (2015), Kunstmuseum St. Gallen (2014) and Haus Esters in Krefeld (2014). Her works have also been on display in numerous group exhibitions, such as Mudam Luxembourg (2015), Bass Museum of Art, Miami Beach (2014), Kunsthalle Wien (2014), Museum of Contemporary Art Detroit (2013), Public Art Fund Exhibition at City Hall Park in New York City (2013), and CCA Wattis Institute, San Francisco (2012). Her works belong to several international private and public collections.

JESSICA MOORE is an author and translator. Her first collection of poems, *EVERYTHING, NOW,* was released with Brick Books in August 2012. She is a former Lannan writer-in-residence and winner of a 2008 PEN America Translation Award for her translation of *TURKANA BOY* by Jean-François Beauchemin. Her poems and translations have appeared in various literary journals in Canada and the US including *THE ANTIGONISH REVIEW, ARC, CAROUSEL, CV2, THE FIDDLEHEAD* and *THE LITERARY REVIEW.*

OTTILIE MULZET is a Hungarian translator of poetry and prose, as well as a literary critic. She has worked as the English-language editor of the internet journal of the Hungarian Cultural Centre in Prague, and her translations appear regularly at Hungarian Literature Online.

TAIYO ONORATO & NICO KREBS, both born 1979 in Switzerland, have collaborated since 2003 and work with photography, film and sculpture. They studied Photography at the ZHDK in Zurich and showed their work in numerous exhibitions in galleries and institutions, among them Kunsthalle Mainz, MaMM Moscow, PS1 MoMA NY, CAC Cincinnati, MocP Chicago, Museum Bellpark, Kunsthaus Aarau, EX3 Firenze. They published *THE GREAT UNREAL* (Edition Patrick Frey, 2009) and *LIGHT OF OTHER DAYS* (Kodoji Press, 2013) and several self-published projects. Their solo show *EURASIA* is on view in Fotomuseum Winterthur until February 12 2016.

DECLAN RYAN was born in Mayo, Ireland and lives in London. A pamphlet of his poems was published in the Faber New Poets series in 2014. He is poetry editor at *AMBIT* and works at King's College, London where he edits wildcourt.co.uk.

LEE SANG-WHA is an emeritus professor in the English Department of Chung Ang University, Seoul, and has published seven volumes of translations of English literature, including two prose works by Gary Snyder.

BROTHER ANTHONY OF TAIZÉ has lived in Korea since 1980. He is an Emeritus Professor at Sogang University, and Chair-Professor at Dankook University. He has published over thirty volumes of English translations of Korean poetry and fiction, including ten volumes of work by Ko Un.

KO UN was born in 1933 in Gunsan, North Jeolla Province, Korea. During the Korean War, he became a monk. Ten years later he returned to the world. After years of dark nihilism, he became a leading spokesman in the struggle for freedom and democracy during the 1970s and 1980s. He has published more than 150 volumes of poems, essays, and fiction. In recent years, more than thirty volumes of translations of his work have been published in some twenty languages.

GABRIELA WIENER (Lima, 1975) is author of the collections of crónicas *LLAMADA PERDIDA*, *SEXOGRAFÍAS*, *NUEVE LUNAS AND MOZART, LA IGUANA CON PRIAPISMO Y OTRAS HISTORIAS*. Her work also includes the poetry collection *EJERCICIOS PARA EL ENDURECIMIENTO DEL ESPÍRITU*. Crónicas of hers have been translated into English, Italian and French. She has lived in Madrid since 2011, where she continues to write for some of the most important magazines and newspapers in America and Europe.

FRIENDS OF THE WHITE REVIEW

JONATHAN CAPE
JONATHAN DUNCAN
JONATHAN WILLIAMS
JORDAN BASS
JORDAN HUMPHREYS
JORDAN RAZAVI
JORDI CARLES SUBIRA
JOSEPH DE LACEY
JOSEPH EDWARD
JOSEPHINE NEW
JOSHUA COHEN
JOSHUA DAVIS
JUDY BIRKBECK
JULIA CRABTREE
JULIA DINAN
JULIE PACHICO
JULIEN BÉZILLE
JURATE GACIONYTE
JUSTIN JAMES WALSH
KAJA MURAWSKA
KAMIYE FURUTA
KATE BRIGGS
KATE LOFTUS-O'BRIEN
KATE WILLS
KATHERINE LOCKTON
KATHERINE RUNDELL
KATHERINE TEMPLAR LEWIS
KATHRYN MARIS
KATHRYN SIEGEL
KEENAN MCCRACKEN
KIERAN CLANCY
KIERAN RID
KIRSTEEN HARDIE
KIT BUCHAN
KYLE PARKER
LAURA SNOAD
LAUREN ELKIN
LEAH SWAIN
LEE JORDAN
LEON DISCHE BECKER
LEWIS BUNGENER
LIA TEN BRINK
LIAM ROGERS
LILI HAMLYN
LILLIPUT PRESS
L'IMPOSSIBLE
LITERARY KITCHEN
LORENZ KLINGEBIEL
LOUISE GUINNESS
LOZANA ROSSENOVA
LUCIA PIETROIUSTI
LUCIE ELVEN
LUCY KUMARA MOORE
LUISA DE LANCASTRE
LUIZA SAUMA
MACK
MACLEHOSE PRESS
MAJDA GAMA
MALTE KOSIAN
MARIA DIMITROVA
MARIANNA SIMNETT
MARILOU TESTARD
MARIS KREIZMAN
MARK EL-KHATIB
MARK KROTOV

MARKUS ZETT
MARTA ARENAL LLORENTE
MARTIN CREED
MARTIN NICHOLAS
MATHILDE CABANAS
MATT GOLD
MATT HURCOMB
MATT MASTRICOVA
MATTHEW BALL
MATTHEW JOHNSTON
MATTHEW PONSFORD
MATTHEW RUDMAN
MAX FARRAR
MAX PORTER
MAX YOUNGMAN
MAXIME DARGAUD-FONS
MEGAN PIPER
MELISSA GOLDBERG
MELVILLE HOUSE
MICHAEL GREENWOLD
MICHAEL HOLTMANN
MICHAEL LEUE
MICHAEL SIGNORELLI
MICHAEL TROUGHTON
MICHELE SNYDER
MILES JOHNSON
MINIMONIOTAKU
MIRIAM GORDIS
MONICA OLIVEIRA
MONICA TIMMS
NAOMI CHANNA
NATHAN BRYANT
NATHAN FRANCIS
NED BEAUMAN
NEDA NEYNSKA
NEIL D.A. STEWART
NEW DIRECTIONS
NICK MULGREW
NICK SKIDMORE
NICK VOSS
NICKY BEAVEN
NICOLA SMYTH
NICOLAS CHAUVIN
NICOLE SIBELET
NILLY VON BAIBUS
OLEKSIY OSNACH
OLGA GROTOVA
OLI JACOBS
OLIVER BASCIANO
OLIVIA HEAL
OLIVIER RICHON
ONEWORLD
ORLANDO WHITFIELD
OSCAR GAYNOR
OWEN BOOTH
ØYSTEIN WARBO
PADDY KELLY
PANGAEA SCULPTORS CENTRE
PATRICK GODDARD
PATRICK HAMM
PATRICK RAMBAUD
PATRICK STAFF
PAUL KEEGAN
PAUL TEASDALE
PEDRO

PEIRENE PRESS
PENGUIN BOOKS
PETER MURRAY
PHILIBERT DE DIVONNE
PHILIP JAMES MAUGHAN
PHILLIP KIM
PHOEBE STUBBS
PICADOR
PIERRE TESTARD
PIERS BARCLAY
PRIMORDIAL SEA
PUSHKIN PRESS
RACHEL ANDREWS
RACHEL GRACE
REBECCA SERVADIO
RENÄTE PRANCÄNE
RENATUS WU
RHYS TIMSON
RICHARD GLUCKMAN
RICHARD WENTWORTH
ROB SHARP
ROB SHERWOOD
ROBERT O'MEARA
ROBIN CAMERON
ROC SANDFORD
RORY O'KEEFFE
ROSALIND FURNESS
ROSANNA BOSCAWEN
ROSE BARCLAY
ROSIE CLARKE
RUBY COWLING
RUPERT CABBELL MANNERS
RUPERT MARTIN
RYAN CHAPMAN
RYAN EYERS
SADIE SMITH
SALLY BAILEY
SALLY MERCER
SALVAGE MAGAZINE
SAM BROWN
SAM GORDON
SAM MOSS
SAM SOLNICK
SAM THORNE
SAMUEL HUNT
SANAM GHARAGOZLOU
SARA BURNS
SARAH HARDIE
SARAH Y. VARNAM
SASKIA VOGEL
SCOTT ESPOSITO
SEAN HOOD
SEB EASTHAM
SELF PUBLISH, BE HAPPY
SERPENTINE GALLERY
SERPENT'S TAIL
SHARMAINE LOVEGROVE
SHOOTER LITERARY MAGAZINE
SIMON HARPER
SIMON WILLIAMS
SIMONE SCHRÖDER
SJOERD KRUIKEMEIER
SK THALE
SKENDER GHILAGA
SOPHIE CUNDALE

FRIENDS OF THE WHITE REVIEW